The ROOFTOP

A Moving Quest for Freedom

Toby Hammerschlag

WOODSLANE PRESS

Woodslane Press Pty Ltd
10 Apollo Street
Warriewood, NSW 2102
Email: info@woodslane.com.au
Tel: 02 8445 2300 Website: www.woodslane.com.au

First published in Australia in 2015 by JoJo Publishing
This edition published in Australia in 2019 by Woodslane Press

ISBN: 978-1-925868-19-7

NATIONAL LIBRARY OF AUSTRALIA
A catalogue record for this book is available from the National Library of Australia

Printed in Australia
Cover image and text images by Kate Chadwick
Book design by Working Type Studio

Dedication

To my beloved grandchildren

DARLINGHURST
EAST SCHOOL

The early mist had lifted to reveal Darlinghurst East Public School sitting in the bright morning light, awaiting the arrival of the students for the first day of the school year. Bordering on the city of Sydney, the school sat wedged between the nearby rich, wooded suburbs and the tall, faceless towers of units and public housing buildings. A damp, sweet smell rose from the newly mown sports-fields, which produced a splash of green between the faded grey classrooms. The school buildings had once been red brick but were now a shade of mouldy grey. Alongside the solid office block, a spiral staircase wound its way up to the rooftop which looked out across Sydney Harbour, where the water shimmered silvery blue on a summer's day but looked grey and menacing when the clouds hung over the city.

The wrought iron front gates with their intricate flower design were unlocked and thrown wide open to welcome the students. The children who lived in nearby leafy Edgecliff and Darling Point, in plush apartments and luxurious houses, began arriving in the latest models of shiny Mercedes, Land Rover and Lexus, which pulled up smoothly and silently to the front gates. They hurriedly waved goodbye to their mothers in their brightly coloured, floral summer dresses and fathers in their neatly pressed suits. At the same time, clapped out Holdens filled with children came to a stop with a grunt. Jostling children poured out of the public school buses that spewed exhaust smoke into the fresh morning air while the rest of the students came sauntering along with their friends. As the students flooded through the school gates, they became an indistinguishable mass of happy schoolmates.

Tuesday Morning:
25 January 2011

The four students sat in an awkward silence in their stiff new uniforms, eagerly awaiting the arrival of their teacher. Every Tuesday, the pupils of Darlinghurst East Public School separated into groups for special classes in Scripture. These four children did not share the same religion but were simply brought together by a friendship that had begun in the playground just three days earlier. The three new students had been standing around self-conscious and alone, feeling swamped by the groups of laughing, running children. Almost imperceptibly, they had moved closer to each other, greeting each other with shy looks and half smiles. Since then, they would search anxiously for each other at the start of school, sit near each other in the classroom and gravitate towards each other at lunch time.

For three of the students, it was not only the beginning of Year 6 but also the start of a new school. Maha Hamdan was new not only to the school but also to Australia. Maha, who had long pitch-black, braided hair and serious brown eyes, sat with her hands folded in her lap. It was as if her life had begun on that September day two years earlier, as the plane started its slow descent into Sydney. Maha had looked through the window at the wide expanse of sea below with growing excitement. The rising sun had painted the ocean in shades of purple and pink and as the plane was nearing landing, she could only just discern the white froth of the breaking waves. At that moment, she had felt the overwhelming desire to jump from her seat and run and shout wildly. But once in Sydney, for two long years Maha had refused to leave her mother's side. It was only in the last few months that Maha had attended a special college for new immigrants to learn English even though since the age of three, her parents had provided her with a tutor in Iraq who taught her English. There were no Islam classes available at this school, so she joined her newfound friends in the Jewish Scripture class.

Sitting next to her was Emma Beaumont. She was the only one among them that had been at the school since kindergarten. Tall, blue-eyed, blonde Emma was an all-rounder. She was not at the top of her class but she did well in her studies and was always in the second highest group for Maths and Reading. She loved sports and participated in all sporting events but netball was definitely her favourite. She had always played the key position of centre and because she was so well liked, she was continuously chosen to be captain of the team year after year. She was not sure why she had been drawn to the three new students in the playground. She had lots of friends but they had looked a little lost and somewhat interesting, or perhaps it was just her good nature that had driven her to approach them on the third day of school.

"Hi, I'm Emma," she had greeted them casually and seen the relief in their eyes at having someone to speak to that was not new to the school.

"Come and I'll show you around," she had offered kindly and they followed her eagerly, taking in their new surroundings. Emma's parents were members of the Uniting Church but only actually attended church at Easter and Christmas. She had decided to join her new friends in the Jewish Scripture class because she wanted to learn about a new religion. She had not asked permission from her parents, knowing that they would approve of her decision.

The third girl in the group was Talia Leveson. Talia had arrived from South Africa two years ago and had, up until now, always attended private schools in both South Africa and Australia. She was tall for her age, ungainly with unruly brown hair that she twirled around her finger constantly to the annoyance of her teachers. Talia had always had difficulties at school. Even in kindergarten, while the other students learnt the names and sounds of letters, Talia was unable to keep them in her head. She was repeatedly sent out of class into small groups which she hated, to be helped with reading and spelling. But what was most difficult for Talia was sitting still and concentrating on what the teacher was saying. Her mind would drift off and her body so wanted to get up and move. It was Talia who had instigated the move to a new school. She had insisted on having a fresh start where nobody knew her or labelled her as 'dumb'. Her parents had initially refused but she had sobbed and screamed until eventually they chose Darlinghurst East as it was known for its caring staff and happy children. Talia was the only Jewish student in this newly formed group.

And then there was Simon Abbot, who had just moved from Melbourne to Sydney with his mum. Simon's mum had wanted to live close to the city and so had chosen to live in Edgecliff as she spent long hours at her job in a large law firm. People would always feel compelled to take a second glance at this young boy with spiky, carrot-red hair, freckled face and pale blue eyes. Simon had a fiery temper and, when angry, would look as if he was about to explode, his face turning to a deeper red than his hair; around his neck always hung a chain with a key to their present apartment. Simon had to move home and city regularly because of Mrs Abbot's job. The chain and key had become an extension of his body and Simon could not remember a time when he had not worn that chain and key, which gave him entry into yet another silent, meticulous apartment. Simon and his mother did not practise any religion, so he had followed his new classmates into the Jewish Scripture class.

The children were startled as a tall, muscular man strode into the room. He was dressed in faded jeans and a crisp white short-sleeved shirt and perched on his long blond-streaked hair was a small woven skullcap. He placed his briefcase on the desk and shifted uneasily on his huge feet. Simon's eyes were transfixed on his bulging arm muscles. Being thin and scrawny himself, which no amount of eating and weightlifting could change, Simon immediately aspired to look like this man. Emma thought that he could easily be a lifesaver on Bondi Beach and wondered what he was doing in the classroom. Talia decided that she had made the right decision in changing schools as no teacher in her previous school had looked even vaguely like him. Maha was feeling slightly intimidated by the size of this man as she had only ever been taught by women. But when she looked into his green eyes speckled with brown, she saw only warmth and kindness and felt reassured.

He began uncertainly, "My name is Mark Zulman. I guess you had better call me Mr Zulman." Four pairs of eyes watched his every move. Unbeknown to the children, this was Mr Zulman's first teaching job and he was feeling rather unsure of himself. Mr Zulman had always wanted to be a teacher. He loved children and from an early age had always been able to weave a story, hiding his shyness

behind a wall of words. He now stood apprehensively before the gaze of the four silent students.

Mr Zulman cleared his throat and, in his nervousness, immediately plunged into the story that he had carefully prepared the night before:

"In the weeks ahead, we are going to travel back 3000 years as if we are in a time capsule to when the Jews, then known as Israelites, had been kept in captivity as slaves for 400 torturous years in Egypt. We arrive at a time when the slaves were still suffering under Pharaoh, king of the Egyptians, who ruled the land with an iron fist. The Jewish festival of Passover, which we are going to learn about, celebrates the liberation or freeing of these slaves and of all people who are oppressed. This is a story for all times, not just a tale to be dusted off and then forgotten. It is a blueprint telling us that every one of us has the right to live in freedom, then and now."

Mr Zulman stopped and ran his fingers through his long, wavy, sun-bleached hair and adjusted his small skullcap. He realised that in his haste to begin, he had forgotten to ask the students their names.

"Before we continue, please tell me your names," he said, looking a little embarrassed.

Simon sat upright in his chair and stuck out his chest, trying to make his small frame larger before this huge man:

"I'm Simon Abbot."

Mr Zulman nodded and looked over at the next student.

"Emma Beaumont," she said brightly and smiled at him.

"Pleased to meet you, Emma," he said and smiled back at her.

"Talia Leveson," Talia announced loudly and with the back of her hand unconsciously pushed back a lock of curly hair that had fallen across her eyes.

"Pleased to meet you also, Talia."

"Maha Hamdan," Maha said softly and did not even look up.

"Now let us start again," Mr Zulman said. "Let's climb back into the time capsule and land in the distant land of Egypt all those years ago."

Mr Zulman took a breath. *Calm down,* he told himself sternly but still launched into his story:

"Pharaoh, king of the Egyptians was a brutal man. To add to the suffering of the slaves, he passed another cruel law decreeing that all male, newborn babies of the Israelites be slain. Can you imagine the terrible suffering of the slaves, especially of the mothers? It is amidst this dark, sad time that a baby boy called Moses was born to a woman called Yocheved. Instead of the birth being a happy time, it was a moment of terrible fear that her newborn baby would be put to death. This distraught mother wept and wept. In a brave attempt to save her baby, Yocheved defied Pharaoh by instructing the baby's sister Miriam to hide him in a waterproof crib in the bulrushes, which are these long reeds that you sometimes see in lakes and rivers. Miriam obeyed her mother and placed his crib gently in the bulrushes keeping guard over her helpless brother. Miriam was gripped with fear when she suddenly saw from her hiding place the arrival of Pharaoh's daughter who had come to bathe near the bulrushes and caught sight of baby Moses. Miriam stayed hidden watching with dread as the princess tenderly lifted the gurgling baby from the crib into her arms. In that moment Miriam knew, even though her heart was breaking, that her brother would be saved if she allowed him to be taken into the safekeeping of the Egyptians. So Moses, child born of an enslaved people, was taken to live in the palace."

Mr Zulman stopped for a moment breathless, realising that he had been speaking non-stop in his nervousness. He looked around at his students and thought that they all looked interested except for Talia, who was fiddling with her pens. Feeling encouraged, he continued:

"The mother and sister of baby Moses, Yocheved and Miriam, were two selfless and brave people who gave up their son and brother to ensure that he was kept alive. Now we all live in Australia, many years later, far removed from that land of oppression; however, we may still have experienced even small acts of kindness by others in our lives. And I am sure that there has been a time when you have put others before yourself. Would anyone like to start by sharing a story where you encountered kindness or perhaps when you have been the person who showed kindness?"

He looked at the students anxiously, wishing for one of them to speak. Maha had tried to follow what Mr Zulman was saying but her English still needed some improvement and some of his words seemed to escape her and she had stopped listening. Her eyes glazed over as she remembered her final night before leaving Iraq. All around her at the airport, there was frantic activity as shouting, sweaty people gathered their precious possessions. She had snuggled into her grandmother's lap and had felt her grandmother's arms wrap around her. Her grandmother's tears had merged with her own as she repeatedly lowered her head to kiss Maha`s face. Then she remembered her father lifting her gently from her grandmother's arms and carrying her to the plane as she wept with her head buried in his shoulder.

As if awakening from a trance, Maha recognised Simon`s voice, "...only see my father every six months as he lives in America. When he comes to Sydney, we spend all our time together. We stay in the Hilton hotel and I'm allowed to order whatever I want from room service. Every morning we drive down to Bronte Beach. My father is a strong swimmer and however fast I swim to try and get away, he always grabs me and throws me under the next wave. Then we go for breakfast on the beachfront and scoff down pancakes with maple syrup. But then his bags are packed and he is ready to go back to Los Angeles. I always feel sad but pretend to smile because I know that my dad will be sad if I am. When I get home, my mum is always grumpy because she hates me spending time with him. So when she asks me if I had a good time, I just say, 'It was ok,' and go to my room."

As Simon finished speaking, he gave a half smile that did not quite reach his eyes. He had wanted to impress Mr Zulman by speaking first and placing himself in a good light. But he now regretted that he had exposed himself. He looked up uncertainly at Mr Zulman, who was nodding his head intently as if every word that he had just said was very important and Simon felt himself relax.

Talia's thoughts had begun to wander while Simon was speaking but she suddenly noticed that the group had become silent and that Mr Zulman was looking directly at her. She looked back at him with surprise. Talia was often forgotten in the rush of overeager students in the crowded classroom, their hands raised and ready to partake while she instead conjured up her next painting in her mind. She looked again into his soft, direct gaze and felt enticed to speak. She began hesitantly, knowing that the story would flow as long as she did not need to write it down. It was always the spelling of the words that made her lose her train of thought.

"Um, for all the time I lived in South Africa, I had a black nanny called Gladys. Every day Gladys would appear just like magic. I never thought to ask her how she got there until I was older. She called me Nyenyane which means 'my precious one' in Sotho, which is an African language. I loved Gladys and still miss her."

Talia's voice quivered. She was surprised that everyone was listening intently to her and so she continued.

"I have always found it difficult to sleep and I still do. I remember my mother insisting when I was little that I take naps and feeling like a prisoner when she shut the door behind her. I would jump up in minutes and hear my mother muttering, 'Never any time for myself'. The door would swing open and there was Gladys with the biggest smile you have ever seen. She had these big white teeth that seemed to shine in her black face," and Talia smiled at the memory.

"'Give her to me, madam!' she would say to my mother and swing me up into her arms. Her arms always felt so strong and she would put me on her back and tie a blanket around us. I remember clearly that the blanket was bright yellow, red and green with a zigzag pattern. I loved the rough feel of it against my cheek. She had this soap smell, not perfumed like my mother's but strong like washing powder. She hummed softly while she did the washing or vacuuming with me on her back and before long I would fall asleep."

Talia could not quite believe that she had told Mr Zulman and the other students about her beloved Gladys. She had always thought that Gladys belonged to her and her alone. *Maybe it is because Mr Zulman is just so cool that I told them*, she thought ruefully to herself.

"Thank you for sharing that with us," Mr Zulman said softly in response. Mr Zulman turned to Maha and asked gently, "Would you like to tell us anything, Maha?" Maha continued to look down at the desk, feeling as if her lips were clamped tightly shut.

He then looked over at Emma, "Would you like to add a story or thought of your own?" he asked quietly.

While Talia had been talking, Emma had been racking her brain for a story to tell but could not for the life of her think of a time that she or her family had made a real sacrifice.

Her family were nothing like Simon`s. Her parents loved each other and did everything together. She remembered her last birthday when she had taken all her friends bowling. Her mother had bought a chocolate ice-cream cake which was decorated with ballerinas, as she loved to dance. She had adored all the attention, especially since her brother and sister were a lot older than her and spoilt her rotten. She looked miserably at her new friends and shook her head.

The bell rang for morning recess and the students jumped up, gathering their belongings and ran out into the playground, barely turning around as Mr Zulman mumbled, "See you next week". Emma noticed Talia taking a skipping rope from her bag. Talia did not particularly like skipping, her timing was always a little off and her feet seemed to get caught in the rope but having a rope insured that she was not left alone. Today she was immediately surrounded by three friends.

"Who wants first turn at holding the rope?" asked Emma.

"Me," said Talia quickly even though she knew that she sometimes struggled to keep an even rhythm. Maha also chose to turn the rope and stood there shyly, concentrating on moving her arm in wide circles. The other two children weaved happily in and out of the rope and were soon joined by other students from their grade.

Tuesday Afternoon

As Maha packed her school bag, she wondered why the end of the school day always seemed to come around so quickly. She loved school and soaked up all the new subjects even though she struggled to understand some of the English words of her teacher with her strong Australian accent.

"G'day" and "Good on you!" she would practise saying to herself in front of the mirror at home but never dared to say these funny sounding phrases aloud at school. Maths was her best subject and she was always the first to finish. She even found herself handing her finished sheet to Talia who struggled with numbers and sat miserably chewing on the end of her pencil during Maths class.

Maha started walking slowly home. She could have caught the bus to nearby Surry Hills but she chose the half-hour walk to avoid as long as possible the responsibilities that always awaited her when she got home. As she arrived home, Maha stood for a moment looking up at the tall, ugly building that they now called home. She could see the many broken window panes covered by cardboard and the torn, dirty, fading cream-coloured net curtains that fluttered in the breeze. The outside area was just a mass of dirt that had turned to dry dust in the summer heat and Maha hated how it stuck to her clothes and shoes. She sighed and entered the foyer of the building. She always held her breath to avoid the stale odour that hung in the lift as it slowly lumbered up the fifteen floors to her unit. Her mother was waiting anxiously for her return in their sparsely furnished unit. The only adornment was the brightly coloured prayer rug in shades of purple and red that lay across the sitting room floor. Her mother was waiting to go shopping with her as she still did not have the confidence to ask in English for what she required and relied on Maha to be her spokesperson. Her mother began to cover her hair with her scarf as she prepared to go out. Maha walked companionably next to her mother and chatted happily in Arabic about her school and her new friends, being careful not to mention the Jewish Scripture class.

They arrived at the local Franklins supermarket and began to do their shopping. Maha knew without being told that they could only afford the cheapest items and she would scour the shelves for home-brands and discounted items. The huge, boisterous Italian man behind the fish counter who had taken a liking to the shy pair greeted them cheerily.

"Hello lovely ladies, today there is a great special on perch fillets and for your smiling faces another ten per cent off!" Maha knew that he was trying to help them and she appreciated his kindness. However, she felt her mother's embarrassment as she shook her head to say 'no' to the offer. Maha scanned the prices, searching for the cheapest fish, "A kilogram, thank you," she said pointing to the bream. He smiled at the timid girl with the strange accent. Maha watched as the fishmonger wrapped up a lot more than one kilogram of bream and hoped that her mother hadn't noticed.

Tuesday Morning: 1 February 2011

The children walked into the tiny room where this time Mr Zulman was already seated at his desk waiting patiently for them. His hair was still damp from his early morning swim on Bondi Beach and he sat with his long legs stretched out under the table. Simon threw an envious glance at Mr Zulman's bulging arm muscles as they settled into their seats. Mr Zulman waited until they were seated comfortably, adjusted his woven skullcap and began to speak:

"As we learnt last week, the Israelites were slaves in Egypt. Pharaoh made them work day and night building his magnificent city. The slaves made the clay for the bricks with their bare hands until their fingers cracked and bled. They groaned in despair as they shuffled along with their backs bent, straining to carry their heavy loads. When they paused, the taskmasters who were hired men to oversee the slaves would beat these tired, starved people. Every day the slaves would weep bitterly and pray that they would be delivered from their endless torment."

Mr Zulman took a breath, stood up and the four children looked up at this colossal man. Even Talia was listening as his words painted pictures in her head of the suffering slaves.

"Pharaoh is the symbol of the force of darkness. Let us go beyond ourselves and think of that darkness spreading its long fingers, gripping the world in the form of harsh rulers who inflict pain and suffering on poor, starved tormented nations."

Mr Zulman stopped for a moment realising he had probably gone a bit overboard with his description.

He continued but this time more simply:

"Taskmasters represent people who carry out evil acts. Even in our own lives, there might be a person who makes our life a misery every single day so that we don't even want to go to school, or perhaps there is a difficulty within ourselves that we struggle with continually."

Mr Zulman spread out large sheets of crisp, white paper on each desk while the students sat in silence, thinking about Mr Zulman's solemn words. He laid out paints in an array of colours and sat down, waiting for them to begin.

"Think about what I have said and just paint whatever comes into your head. Anything goes!"

Mr Zulman noticed that Maha was looking at him in confusion. He felt a pang of guilt at having being caught up in his own descriptions without having considered Maha's English skills.

"What I am saying, Maha is that like the slaves, we may have experienced sadness in our lives or we might still be feeling pain within ourselves, even today..." Mr Zulman's voice trailed off as he saw the flash of anguish in Maha's eyes and he regretted having asked her to revisit her past.

He added quickly, "Only if you want to, Maha."

She looked into the distance for a moment then carefully picked up a black texta and began to draw.

Talia, who was usually the last to begin any task, had already started painting. Talia loved art and knew that while she struggled to write down her thoughts, she could easily draw her ideas since pictures just seemed to pop into her head. She drew an oversized teacher figure bending menacingly over a little girl seated at her desk. She drew the teacher with an ugly mouth and protruding eyes. She dipped her brush in the brown paint and began to paint the little girl's brown curls falling across her face. She stopped for a moment and surveyed the scene on her paper. She picked up a thin paintbrush, dipped it carefully into the emerald green paint and started to paint the hair ribbons as if trying to tie back the stubborn curls. She continued to draw carefully but no one could see the face of the girl with teary eyes as she stared sadly down at the book in front of her with the letters jumping all over the page.

While the others followed Talia's lead and also began to paint, Emma sat frozen in her seat. She stared at the blank white paper in front of her, which seemed as empty as her life. *Why did I even join this class*? she wondered dejectedly. "Fingers of darkness!" she repeated Mr Zulman's words to herself with disdain, "he speaks like a man straight out of the Bible. I am being punished for being happy!" Emma looked over at Simon's painting. She saw that he had drawn a little boy with red hair whom she immediately identified as Simon himself standing dwarfed between two tall people, a woman and a man with large gaping, shouting mouths. She watched intrigued as he dipped his brush into the red paint and spread it onto the boy's face. The face was curdling with anger. She could feel the misery as he drew their outstretched hands pulling the boy apart.

Emma sat despondently in the quiet of the classroom. Her eyes fell on Maha's sheet. To her shock, she saw no colour at all. Maha was using only black paint. Emma watched as Maha drew a large room with row after row of beds against the pristine white paper. Emma was not sure what it all meant but she had to turn away, while her empty paper stared back at her accusingly.

At last the bell rang for morning recess. For Emma,

the last thirty minutes had seemed like an eternity. She sprang from her seat, took one last regretful glance at the untouched white sheet and made for the door. The others followed her out of the classroom and although it was still early in the day, they felt the mounting heat. As they were about to pass the office building, Simon whispered to the others, "Let's climb to the rooftop to eat our morning tea."

Talia and Maha hesitated. The rooftop was out of bounds to the students. Having just started at a new school, they didn't want to break the rules. Emma, in all her years at the school, had not even considered the possibility of climbing to the rooftop. They looked uncertainly at the staircase encrusted with flakes of rust. Simon looked around and urged them, "C'mon there's no one around, follow me!" They reluctantly followed him, quickly climbing the creaky stairs while constantly glancing over their shoulders.

As they stepped onto the rooftop, they were immediately rewarded by the soft, cool breeze that swept off the harbour. They stood for a moment enjoying the view of the sailing boats which looked like white frozen dots on the still water. While the others sat down, Maha shaded her eyes and stood motionless staring at the Opera House. She squinted and thought that it looked like a huge sailing boat billowing in the wind while wisps of cloud hovered above and she almost expected it to sail away into the distance.

"Maha!" she heard Emma call and she turned and sat down beside them.

They opened their brown paper morning-tea bags while Maha opened one of her two lunch boxes that her mother insisted on sending with her each day. Her lunch boxes were always a source of fascination for the other children. The three friends cast inquisitive side glances into the box. Today there was flat bread filled to overflowing with neatly chopped salad. The smell of garlic was overpowering but that did not diminish their curiosity.

Maha, sensing their interest and having been taught the importance of sharing, offered her food to the others. "Would you like some?" she asked, handing over her lunch box.

"Sure would! Let's swap," replied Simon eagerly and he and Emma offered their chips, muesli bars and apples in exchange. As they bit into the pitta bread, they were quite taken aback by the sudden hit of spicy hummus but munched away happily, enjoying the tingle on their tongues.

"Once had felafel on Bondi Beach with my dad," Simon told Maha, while wiping the dripping hummus off his chin with the back of his hand.

"Really?" said Maha with some surprise while thinking that it was very strange that her country's food was sold near a beach in Sydney. She bit gingerly into the muesli bar and immediately liked the sweet taste so early in the morning. Talia reluctantly declined to exchange her morning tea. Her mother had placed her on a special diet with the start of her new school. She knew that it was supposed to help her concentrate and she was not sure if Maha`s food fitted into her new diet, so she miserably ate her fresh fruit while watching the others intently with envy.

Tuesday Afternoon

Whenever the school day ended, Simon hated the thought of returning directly to the apartment where nobody was home and only silence greeted him in the rambling unit. Leaving the schoolyard, he kicked a few stones as he strolled aimlessly along. It had become a habit for him to stop on his way home from school at Mr Naidoo's shop. He had first noticed the shop a few days after arriving in Sydney as he ambled home from school trying to familiarise himself with the best route home. It was the strong smell of curry that wafted out onto the street that first attracted him. To his delight, the shop was an intriguing combination of a newsagency, grocery store and deli. Behind the counter stood Mrs Naidoo providing a flash of colour in her bright pink sari. Mr Naidoo had noticed the tell-tale sign of the key around his neck, which told him that no-one would be waiting for Simon and invited him into the shop.

"Sit, sit my boy," he had welcomed him warmly while pulling out a stool from under the counter.

Today Simon settled himself on the same stool behind the counter, helped himself to a samousa, whose spicy taste made his eyes water and began to tell Mr Naidoo about his new friends.

"One girl, Talia, is from South Africa, and the other girl Maha is from...I don't know where," he began while Mr Naidoo listened and continued to serve customers. While he was talking, he was interrupted by the ring of his mobile phone and knew that it would be his mother, who called him every day at the same time to check that he was safely home.

"Nearly home," he lied.

"Well hurry up!" she responded grumpily. He could detect the impatience in her voice and knew with certainty that it would be hours before she would finally arrive home from work, bringing with her takeaway for their dinner. He shoved the phone into his pocket and turned his attention back to Mr Naidoo, "As I was saying..." and helped himself to another samousa.

Tuesday Morning: 8 February 2011

Like the very first class, the children sat waiting for Mr Zulman. On Emma's desk was a rolled up sheet of white paper. They all looked at it with curiosity. Emma remained tight-lipped while the elastic band closed around it tightly held her secret.

Mr Zulman came rushing in, flustered and muttering, "Sorry I'm late."

The students smiled to themselves as they noted his damp hair with his skullcap askew and the fine sea sand still stubbornly clinging to his arms. They guessed correctly that he must have forgotten the time while swimming in the ocean.

Emma ceremoniously began to unroll her sheet of paper and the others gathered around. Mr Zulman was relieved that the attention was on Emma, which gave him a small reprieve to get his thoughts in order before having to start teaching.

"I know I can't paint like Talia, so I drew stick figures

for my story. This isn't my own story. It is made up and not made up, if you know what I mean," explained Emma.

Mr Zulman and the others moved closer to her to get a better look at the busy page.

"I will point and tell the story like in a comic."

"Pull up your chairs," suggested Mr Zulman, "so that we can look and listen."

Emma remained standing and used a pencil to point at each block as she told the story.

"The year is 1950. That is the father. He took his billycan, threw his duffel bag over his shoulder and walked towards the hills to look for work. There is the mother standing with her hands on her hips, watching him but he does not turn around. The older black girl is playing in the red sand with her little sister."

Emma stopped for a moment and added, "I was in Alice Springs last year and the sand there is fine and red."

No one moved or commented, so she continued.

"The sun is blazing and reflects off the tin humpy, so the girl has to shade her eyes when she hears the screech of the wheels of the ute. She hears the mother shouting, 'Run, run!' She jumps up trying to drag her sister with her but it is too late. The strong white men grab the little black girl. She kicks and bites but they are too strong and they shove her into the back of the ute."

Emma took a breath and still no-one moved.

"Here she is standing in the market place with the other black girls. The big farmer and his wife choose her. I just realised that I did not give her a name. Not sure of Aboriginal names!"

No one responded or even made a suggestion.

"Here," she continues to explain, "they are taking her to their farm. She sits alone in the back of the truck. They make her their slave. She gets up before the sun rises and lights the big coal stove. See, there she is dragging the bags of coal. Here she is scrubbing the floor and washing the clothes until her hands are dry and cracked. It is dark when she lies down on the hard straw in the shed. She is exhausted but still wonders about her mum and sister."

Everyone remained silent until Mr Zulman said softly, "I see you are talking about the 'stolen generation', Emma."

He turned to Maha, "For many years, the Aboriginal children in Australia were taken from their mothers with a promise of a better life but this mostly didn't happen."

The other students stared back at him with shock.

"That is such a sad story, Mr Zulman," said Talia with a catch in her voice. "Did it really happen?"

"Laws were passed about fifty years ago to stop this practice," he replied, "but yes it did happen for decades."

Emma rolled up her drawing while the others walked

slowly back to their seats. The sadness of the story hung in the air. Mr Zulman stood pensively, looking at his students for a few moments. They looked back at him, all very serious. He did not want his students to always leave his class feeling sad and he was just a little afraid that they might not return the following week.

"Let us try and turn our minds away from the gloom of Emma's story and travel back to Egypt but this time to a much happier place," he said.

He tried to smile cheerfully at the students and they smiled back tentatively.

"Moses was living in the palace as a prince distanced from the torment of his people," he began. "He had beautiful clothes made from soft velvet and woven from the finest silk. He had a tutor that would come to teach him and he ate his food served from shiny silver platters. He even had his own personal servant that would hover near him to tend to his every need."

The bell would ring soon and Mr Zulman really wanted them to leave his class feeling happy, for once.

"Take a few minutes, close your eyes and place yourself with Moses in the luxury of the palace. It doesn't have to be a typical palace. It can be your own idea of a palace."

The moment that Emma closed her eyes, she had an image of Moses at Hayman Island in Queensland where she had holidayed in the summer. *For once, I can be part of this class,* she thought, relieved. She saw herself sitting next to Moses at breakfast, their plates laden with her favourite freshly baked soft pastry oozing with custard. When the tide receded, she walked out to the ocean with him and she felt the soft, wet sand squelching between her toes. When they began to feel tired, they stretched out on lounges next to the one of the winding swimming pools. A waiter served them mocktails in long iced glasses laden with sliced strawberries and finished off with little purple paper umbrellas perched on sweet-smelling pineapple pieces balancing on the edge of the glasses.

Simon sat next to Emma with his eyes tightly shut. The picture that had immediately arisen for Simon was of his father's house on Malibu Beach in California. He eliminated his stepmother and stepsisters from the scene and placed himself and Moses on the beach playing cricket with his father and mother, whom he reunited in his imagination. On the beach stood a huge battery-operated freezer with scrumptious chocolate-coated vanilla ice-creams with cookie dough. The burning sun beat down faster than they could lick their ice-creams and they had to stick their tongues out to catch the melted chocolate before it dripped down their chins. He ran with Moses, who was still wearing his crown, into the tumbling waves while his parents stood hand-in-hand happily watching from the beach.

Talia laid her head on the desk and closed her eyes. *I know exactly where I am going to take Moses,* Talia thought to herself. "Better than any palace. I am going to take him to the back steps of our veranda, where I used to sit with my nanny Gladys when Mum was out." She placed Gladys between her and Moses. She remembered how Gladys would sigh as she heaved the black iron pot between them.

"Go for it! And use your hands. It is what is called *pap,* made from maize," she told Moses.

Talia could feel the spongy, white porridge squishing in her hand as she formed it into a ball and dipped it into the thick, spicy tomato gravy and then crammed it into her mouth. Eating this food had been forbidden to Talia by her mother as she said that it was unhealthy and she laughed to herself at how she had to clean up every speck of food before her mother returned home.

Maha did not need to close her eyes. A palace for her was the family estate in which they had lived in Baghdad before the time when their lives had changed forever. She remembered with intense pleasure the Persian rugs with their intricate designs carefully laid across the newly washed stone floors and their carved cedar furniture which was hundreds of years old, handed down from generation to generation. She placed Moses sitting outside in the shade of one of the many palm trees sipping cold pomegranate juice. She could taste the bittersweet red liquid. Through Moses' eyes, she surveyed the olive groves that stretched out as far as the eye could see, the branches heavy with plump, black olives. Maha heard the children moving around her and so she stood up reluctantly not wanting to leave the place to which she had gone.

It was already ten minutes into morning recess when the children filed out of the classroom. "Let's go to the roof again," said Simon excitedly and they followed him up the staircase with only a few swift backward glances this time. As they reached the last step, the strong wind almost knocked them over, so they had to hold onto the rails.

"Let's go into the playground," suggested Talia, who was feeling a little frightened, as she hated feeling off balance.

"No!" was the quick response from Maha and they all turned to look at her in surprise. Maha blushed, "It's just that I like it up here," she tried to explain.

"That's OK," responded Talia placatingly as they took shelter behind a huge pillar.

They watched as Maha made her way forward unsteadily until she grabbed tightly onto the barrier. She looked out across the harbour. The sea was agitated and the boats were tugging to be set free from their anchors. Maha unloosened her hair from the tight grip of the elastic and faced directly into the wind, letting her hair fly in all directions. The others nibbled at their morning tea while their eyes stayed fixed on the windblown figure. When Maha finally came to join them, she seemed far away. She sat wrapped in her own world and did not offer them her food, nor did they ask for any.

Tuesday Afternoon

As soon as the final bell of the day sounded, Talia was expected to walk straight to her mother's waiting car. She had continuously begged her mother to allow her to catch the bus home but her mum had flatly refused. Talia heaved her heavy school bag overflowing with books onto her shoulder. She had simply not bothered to find out which books she needed in order to do her homework and before her teacher could help her, she had stuffed all of them into her bag and quickly left the classroom. She saw her mum sitting ramrod straight in her silver Lexus waiting for her to emerge from the school gates. Mrs Leveson always tried to arrive early in order to park closest to the gate. It annoyed Talia that her mother was always there, never giving her the chance to linger and chat to any of her friends.

"She is like a sergeant major," Talia grumbled to herself.

She threw her heavy bag onto the back seat with a thump and some of the books fell out. Talia saw the flash of annoyance on her mother's face.

In a soft but stern voice, Mrs Leveson began to admonish

Talia, "How many times have we discussed that you need to sort your books before leaving the classroom?"

Talia simply ignored her, changed the radio station to 104.1FM and turned up the volume. Her mum crossly turned down the volume and put her foot on the accelerator.

They sat in silence for the journey home with only the beat of the music filling the space between them until the car weaved up the winding driveway to their imposing two-storey Vaucluse house. Mrs Leveson was clearly frustrated with her daughter and Talia was sick of hearing her mum's complaints. The towering glass windows of Talia's house looked out onto North Head but Talia didn't care about the view of the imposing cliffs and lapping waves. It was always a race against time to watch as much television as possible before having to start her homework. She could feel her anxiety growing and the muscles tightening in the pit of her stomach.

She grabbed her afternoon tea that was carefully laid out on a plate and sat down on a stool in the kitchen as this was the only place that she was allowed to eat.

"Boring, boring," she mumbled as she viewed the salad sandwich and thinly sliced apple and oranges. She thought enviously of Maha and Simon. She was sure that Maha's mother would prepare something exotic for afternoon tea that would make her tongue tingle. Or even better, Simon had told her that he always had money to buy himself a treat on his way home, which was usually a chocolate bar or ice-cream. Talia glanced around the kitchen as she gobbled down her food. The bench tops, like the rest of the house, were always sparkling clean. Her mother abhorred mess and Talia's shoes and clothes that were always strewn across her bedroom floor made her mother turn white with rage. Talia dusted the crumbs off her lap when her mother wasn't looking and quickly placed her plate in the dishwasher.

She switched on the television and, not before long, became engrossed in Nickelodeon, which was her favourite afternoon channel. It felt like it had only been a few minutes before she heard her mother's quiet, determined voice, "Talia, time to switch off the TV and start your homework!"

Pretending not to hear, Talia just continued to watch her program. She heard the click of the remote and reluctantly stood up and made her way to the table where her mum had already sorted and arranged her books. The long afternoon began with Talia chewing on the end of her pen while her mind wandered. She wished that she was hundreds of kilometres away with Moses in a distant land. Her daydream didn't last long as she was brought back to reality with a start by her mother's sharp command, "Talia, concentrate!"

Tuesday Morning:
15 February 2011

Mr Zulman was leaning against the classroom wall when they arrived. His presence seemed to fill the room. It was as if he was too large for the space and that he was better suited to being outdoors. He smiled at his students warmly and Talia thought to herself that she loved the way his skin crinkled in the corners of his eyes. They settled into their seats and waited expectantly for him to begin.

"Last week, we spoke briefly of young Moses and how he grew up in the luxury of Pharaoh's palace. One day he was taking a walk outside the palace and saw an Egyptian brutally beating an Israelite slave. He could have continued to walk and just ignore this cruelty but Moses became enraged by this ruthless person. He grabbed the whip from the hand of the Egyptian taskmaster and struck the cruel taskmaster with it. Moses became fearful that his life might be in grave danger from what he had just done, so he fled from the comfort of the grand palace into the harsh wilderness.

"I remind you all that this story took place a very, very long time ago. However, throughout history and even up to the present day, there are brave people who sacrifice their own lives to aid the cause of others or use their power to protect people who are more vulnerable than themselves. Is there a person that you have heard of or know, or even you yourself, that has personally intervened on behalf of the less fortunate?"

Before anyone could respond, they heard a gulp and all eyes turned to Maha, who had tears streaming down her cheeks. She was desperately trying not to sob. Mr Zulman got up and concernedly bent over her, his large frame dwarfing that of the girl, "Maha, are you all right?"

There was no response from Maha. Her silence was broken by Simon, who surprised even himself by beginning to speak. It was as if a flood of words started pouring out of him and he could not stifle their flow.

"When I was eight, my parents decided to get divorced. My father wanted me to live with him in America but my mum wanted me to stay with her in Australia. While they lived together, they fought all the time and sometimes I'd have to cover my ears to block out their screaming. Then one day we had to go to court. The judge was an old man. We went to his chambers, which are just like an office. When we arrived, he was sitting at a huge desk, wearing his wig and a black cloak like you see in the movies. As soon as he saw us, he took off his wig and I was surprised to see that he was completely bald. I wanted to laugh but everyone was so serious, so I tried my best not to. I sat between my parents. They both looked sad and angry. The judge looked at some papers on his desk and then looked up at me. He got up and came around to us from his desk. I felt scared, just a little actually, but I tried not to show it. The judge told me that he was there to help me. He asked me what I liked doing and what I did with my mum and what I did with my dad. I told him that my dad was a great soccer player and that he always took me to the park and we ran around kicking the ball. Mum was always busy at work but she made the best choc-chip muffins and always allowed me to nibble on the choc-chips while she was baking. And then he asked me whether I wanted to live with Dad or Mum. I started to cry and said that I wanted to live with both of them." Simon stopped and quickly added, "I was little then and would not cry now, of course!"

"The judge dug into his pocket and handed me a huge, white handkerchief and told me not to worry and that he would make sure that I would be with both my mum and dad. He kept his word. I live with my mum most of the time and every holiday my dad visits me or I visit him in Los Angeles."

As Simon's surge of words came to an abrupt halt, an uncomfortable silence descended on the room. Simon turned bright red. He had never spoken about that day before and was not quite sure why he had felt the need to share that very private part of his life with his classmates and teacher.

What is it about Mr Zulman that always makes me want to talk? he chided himself and then thought gratefully, *at least there are no boys in the class. They would have thought I was a wuss!*

Mr Zulman stood up and placed a hand on Simon's shoulder. His hand was heavy but strong and Simon felt strangely comforted.

"Thank you so much for sharing that experience with the class, Simon. The judge was indeed a man like Moses, who cared about the needs of others."

The bell for morning recess rang and before Mr Zulman could say anything further, the students grabbed their books and hurriedly left the classroom. Simon, who had begun to feel acutely embarrassed in front of his classmates, ran off without a backward glance. The girls did not even consider climbing to the rooftop without Simon and walked over to sit in the shade of the peppertree with its soft, overhanging branches to eat their morning tea.

Tuesday Afternoon

The final school bell rang. Emma was excited as it was trials for the netball team. She had asked Talia and Maha if they wanted to join her but Talia had just laughed and said, "No one would want me on their team. I can't catch a ball to save my life!" Maha had said that she didn't know what netball was but would come and watch for a short time as her mum was expecting her home.

The girls stood waiting excitedly but with a little trepidation for the sports teacher to arrive. Ms Nixon was a no-nonsense coach who had the reputation of being very tough but she believed strongly in fair play and in giving everyone 'a go'. No one could remember her not being at the school and her weather-beaten face appeared as worn as the surrounding buildings. With the passing of time, her once trim body had become increasingly large and rounded but her booming voice had not diminished. She arrived in her bright red tracksuit, dragging a string bag filled with netballs.

"Two lines facing each other!" she bellowed without

bothering to greet the children. The girls began to throw the balls back and forth to each other.

"You!" she shouted at Maha, who was sitting on the sideline, engrossed in watching the practice. "Don't just stand there like a stunned mullet. Join a line and eye on the ball!" Maha had not quite understood what Ms Nixon was saying but before she could even respond, she was standing next to Emma and anticipating catching the next ball.

Half an hour later, all the girls were placed in positions on the court. Emma, as usual, was chosen as centre while Maha was given the position of goal shooter and told to stand under the goalpost. Emma quickly tried to explain to Maha that it was her role to shoot the ball into the ring and her departing words were, "You're only allowed one step when you are holding the ball". Ms Nixon blew the whistle and play began. Maha was amazed at how fast Emma could move and how high she could jump when she was trying to intercept the ball. But what surprised Maha even more was that every time Emma passed the ball to her, she could actually shoot the ball into the ring, or very close to it. When the ball went into the ring, everyone on her team would cheer. Maha was having so much fun that when she glanced at her watch; a whole hour had already elapsed. She knew that her mother would be hysterical. She ran frantically off the court and all Ms Nixon could hear between Maha's panicked breaths were the words "got to... home...worried..." as she ran towards the gate. Ms Nixon was speechless as no child had ever dared run off without permission in her twenty years of teaching.

Maha could hardly breathe as she turned the key in the door. Through the corner of her eye, she saw the bucket, mop and vacuum and knew that her father was home. She also knew that she was in deep trouble as soon as she saw her mother's tear-stained face. Her mother saw her and immediately started screaming wildly in Arabic while hugging her to her chest.

"I was playing netball and forgot the time," she tried to explain but could not be heard above her mother's sobs.

Her father admonished her quietly saying, "Maha, you have been very inconsiderate. You know how much your mother has been through. If you ever come home late, we need to be told. No excuses."

Maha nodded, feeling deeply remorseful, her eyes brimming with tears.

*

Back on the netball court, Ms Nixon blew the final whistle to mark the end of the netball trials. Emma slung her schoolbag over her shoulder and noticed her mum waiting for her at the school gate while happily chatting to the other mums. As Emma approached her, Mrs Beaumont took the heavy schoolbag from her and gave her a quick hug.

"Ooh, sweaty Emma, you must have played hard."

Emma didn't respond and made her way to the parked car. Mrs Beaumont handed Emma her favourite treat, which was a doughnut with pink icing and a berry juice. She sunk her teeth into the soft dough as her mum started the car. Her mum looked over at her with concern.

"Emma, what's the matter? You are usually so hyped up after netball trials!"

Emma continued to munch on her doughnut while intermittently sipping her juice.

She began hesitantly, "Mum, you remember how I told you about the Jewish Scripture class that I joined?"

"I certainly do," replied Mrs Beaumont.

"Well, I really like these guys. They're all kind of different," continued Emma, "but today the boy Simon told us about his parents' divorce and it really made me sad. And then the girl Maha, who I think is from Iraq, came to netball. She was having a great time. I even saw her smile and she never smiles. And she was really good at shooting even though she had never played netball before. Then all of a sudden she just ran off the court..."

Emma continued to mumble to herself, "I just don't get it. I don't get any of it. Maybe I shouldn't even be in that class!"

Her mum nodded sympathetically, choosing her words carefully, "You know, Em, people come from all kinds of different worlds and different backgrounds. But I am really proud that you have befriended these kids. You might learn a few valuable life lessons from them and I am quite sure that they will benefit from your friendship too."

They continued the short trip home in companionable silence until Mrs Beaumont pulled into their driveway in a tree-lined street in Paddington where the houses nestled close to each other. Emma jumped out of the car, went straight to the kitchen, rummaged through the fridge, found some leftover chicken and salad, which she slapped between two slices of bread and plonked herself on the couch in front of the television. She threw off her shoes and made herself comfortable amidst the large comfy cushions. Her golden Labrador, Cooper, jumped up onto the couch and snuggled up next to her. She popped little bits of her sandwich into Cooper's mouth as she watched television.

Tuesday Morning: 22 February 2011

The girls were already seated when Simon arrived. During the week after telling his story, he had avoided all contact with the girls. Even when Talia was struggling in Maths class, he didn't lean over surreptitiously and pass her his maths sheet. He did notice, however, that Maha was even quieter than usual as she passed her finished maths sheet to Talia who, with a quick glance to check that the teacher wasn't watching, gleefully copied all the answers as speedily as she could.

There was a whiff of the salty ocean as Mr Zulman came rushing in. He immediately noticed that they were all sitting without talking. He looked at his students curiously. His eyes rested on Maha who, for the first time, was looking directly at him with her brown doe-like eyes. He smiled at her kindly and turned to his other students, "I have been thinking of Simon's story the whole week…" but he did not finish his sentence because when he glanced over at Simon, he saw that his face was bright red. Mr Zulman realised that he should have just moved on with the story of Moses and was very upset with himself for having caused Simon further embarrassment.

Before Mr Zulman could continue, he was interrupted by the soft voice of Maha. Even though Maha's English was adequate and improving every day, she seemed to struggle to find the right words.

"I also like to tell a little of my story."

She stopped and Mr Zulman was not sure if she would continue. Maha looked at Mr Zulman as if seeking reassurance.

He looked directly back at her and said, "We would very much like to hear what you have to say." And his words were spoken as softly as hers and so she continued.

"My father, he was a very clever doctor in Iraq. People, they come from far towns to see him. People were always at the side of our house waiting for him. Father, he also travelled all over Iraq to help people. My mother, she was very scared. She said to my father that he must not go far, too much danger. But Father, he kept saying that he is a doctor, his job is to help people everywhere."

A heavy feeling of foreboding hung in the air and the others held their breath, not knowing what was coming next. Even Talia did not move. Maha looked again at Mr

Zulman and spoke so softly that the others had to move closer to hear her.

"One day Father was at a hospital in a town called Hilla. Father was walking to his car," Maha's voice faded to barely a whisper, "There was a big bomb in the car park," and for a moment she did not speak.

"Father was in hospital for a long time. Mother cried all the time. His hands they were broken, no more doctor, no more work. Father said we must come to Australia. But Australia did not want my family." Maha stopped for a moment and then added quietly, "We are still not sure if Australia wants us!"

Emma immediately thought of the long room and rows of beds in Maha's painting and it all became clear to her. The others sat numb with shock.

Emma was the first to recover. "We want you," she said gently.

Maha turned to Emma with a radiant smile, unexpectedly changing the subject, "Father says I can play netball if I always tell Mother where I am."

Still reeling from Maha's story, Emma turned to her and mumbled, "That's great, you're going to be really good."

When the others looked at Mr Zulman, they saw that his eyes had filled with tears. He could not speak for a few seconds. He rubbed away the tears with the back of his hand, swallowed hard, cleared his throat and said, "Maha, thank you, thank you." And for once, words did not come easily to him.

"You have taught us that there are people who are still experiencing terrible suffering and hardship in the world. But there are always good people like your father who will help others at whatever cost." He gulped and his deep voice seemed to crack, "Maha, I am sorry for your pain." He stopped and the students had to look away from this giant of a man who, for the first time, had spoken so simply in his concern for Maha. After a few minutes, he managed to continue and his tone was lighter, "I would like to refocus our attention on Moses."

He took a breath and began slowly:

"Our story is now changing as we see the shimmer of the light of freedom."

He looked directly at Maha as if wanting to shine the light of hope directly on her but not before long, he was lost in his own world of words.

"We know that Moses had to flee into the wilderness when he killed the taskmaster. It was in the wilderness that Moses was taken in by a man called Jethro and then married his daughter Zippora. One day Moses was walking on a mountain, tending Jethro's sheep, when suddenly before him a bush was ablaze with huge orange flames.

Now as we know in Australia, a bushfire can spread rapidly, destroying everything in its path. However, this bush did not burn despite being on fire. The angel of God was amidst the flames. The light of the flames can be seen as the symbol of hope when we, like Moses, are surrounded by darkness."

Again he stopped and looked at Maha. She looked back at him, not quite understanding all that he was saying but the sound of his words nonetheless washed over her and soothed her.

"It is a reminder that when bleakness and despair envelop us, we must keep the flame of hope burning. God commanded Moses to confront Pharaoh and ordered him to free the Israelite slaves. Moses was afraid. But God instructed Moses to go forth with his brother Aaron as his spokesman and to order Pharaoh to 'Let my people go!' This is a command or slogan for all times and for all people who are oppressed to demand to be set free."

The bell rang. The students were so immersed in the story that they did not move. After a pause, they reluctantly got up and started making their way out to morning recess. Talia put her arm companionably through Maha's, surprising herself as she hated being touched or touching others, "I'm happy to have you here as our friend," she said and smiled at the downcast Maha.

"Yeah," echoed Simon.

"Now we can play netball together!" shouted Emma, jumping up and pretending to catch a ball.

Maha's frown was transformed into a beaming smile. "I'll play like a tiger," she responded and they smiled back at her as they made their way up to the roof. They stood for a moment, pensively looking out across the harbour at the wide expanse of water that today lay still without even a ripple. They sat down, enjoying the quiet of the rooftop, wanting to banish the horror of Maha's story.

Talia had seen Ms Nixon from afar in the playground. Talia knew that she was hopeless at ball sports. She simply could not coordinate her eyes and hands however hard she tried but she desperately wanted to be on the netball court with her friends.

"Be back in a minute," she said to her friends and made her way down the wobbly staircase and began to walk resolutely towards Ms Nixon. As she drew closer, she began to falter.

Talia continued walking slowly towards her, unsure as to what she was going to say until she found herself cowering before her.

"What can I do for you?" Ms Nixon asked her in a brisk tone that made her even more fearful.

"I... I was just wondering," she stammered, for once at a loss for words.

"Speak up, girl," boomed Ms Nixon.

Talia continued uncertainly, "I can't catch a ball but I really want to play netball with my friends."

Ms Nixon looked at her scornfully, "Everyone can catch a ball. I'll see you this afternoon, now scram!"

Talia ran off happily to call her mum and ask for her permission. Her mum was so surprised by the news that she agreed. Mrs Leveson was still mid-sentence saying, "... you will still have to do all you homework when..." but Talia had already hung up and was climbing excitedly back up the staircase to the rooftop to tell her friends.

Tuesday Afternoon

It had been a sweltering day and the overhead fans were whirring furiously, providing little relief to the hot and restless kids. Talia just couldn't concentrate with that constant buzz above her. As the school day drew to an end, she began to regret her hasty decision to play netball, fearing that she would embarrass herself in front of her friends. But half an hour before the end of school, the sky began to darken as heavy black clouds crept rapidly over the blue sky and hung threateningly waiting to burst. Talia felt secretly relieved. She was sure that netball would be cancelled and she would not have to catch that wretched ball. The skies opened and rain fell heavily down and thundered on the tin roof. Emma looked bitterly disappointed but then the sky cleared; the sun shone once again and humidity hung in the air.

As they assembled on the netball court, steam was rising from the asphalt surface. Even before they started playing, their clothes clung to them in the sweltering heat and Talia was covered in the sweat of humidity and fear. Emma picked up the ball and started throwing it back and forth with Maha. Maha, who was usually so self-contained, was jumping up and down with excitement. Talia stood self-consciously in her school shoes, incredulously watching Emma's swivelling feet. While the girls were gathering on the netball court, Simon came sauntering by. He noticed his three friends on the netball court amidst the multitude of girls. He looked over at the adjacent field where the boys had gathered for soccer practice. He always played soccer with his father, so it was just too painful a reminder of their time together to play when his father was so far away in America. He thought to himself, *Mum always says that a woman can do anything a man can do, so surely the opposite is also true.*

By this time, the huge figure of Ms Nixon had arrived, dragging behind her a huge bag of balls. The girls began to gather around her.

"Form a circle!" she bellowed.

Maha wondered why Ms Nixon had to scream when her mere presence made everyone quiet.

Simon's hesitancy only lasted a few seconds as he dropped his bag and ran up to Ms Nixon.

"Ms Nixon, can I also play netball?"

Ms Nixon looked at him with interest. She had never had this request from a boy before. She didn't bother to reply to his question and Simon had to step back as she shouted,

"Name?"

"Simon."

"Join a line!"

Simon quickly messaged his mum on his mobile phone to tell her that he would be home late from school and ran to join a line. He grinned happily at Talia, who was standing at the end of the line.

That's all I need, thought Talia. *Now Simon will also see how bad I am!*

Ms Nixon blew hard into her whistle above the excited chatter of the players and they started throwing the balls back and forth. Emma caught and threw with ease, as did Maha. Simon also had no trouble catching and although he had no idea how to do a netball throw, he observed the girls and mastered it within a very short time. For Talia, the dreaded ball seemed to come faster and faster towards her, evading her waiting hands. The sweat poured off her forehead. Ms Nixon placed herself behind Talia, which just added to her nervousness.

"Eye on the ball. Get ready, arms out, now catch!" she shouted.

But still the ball bypassed her outstretched hands. Ms Nixon was flummoxed; she had never seen a girl that could not catch a single ball. Despite her gruff manner, she felt bad for this young girl who had sweat pouring down her

face and respected her effort. There was no chance that she would be able to hold her own in a team.

Then an idea struck her, "Talia, we need a manager as much as we need players for this team. Are you organised?"

Relief flooded over Talia.

"Definitely," she lied happily. "And can I paint banners too?"

"Absolutely," replied Ms Nixon with as much relief as Talia, while secretly congratulating herself on her ingenuity.

"Meet your new manager," she announced loudly to the other girls and Simon and, pointing to Talia, said, "We will discuss your duties after practice and in the meantime get yourself a drink."

Talia made her way to the tap, realising that she was parched.

"I'll be so organised and the team will have the best banners," she promised herself. Already her mind was envisioning background colours and lettering. Emma, Maha and Simon were delighted. They had watched their friend's embarrassment and had been at a loss at how to help her.

Talia sat happily on the sideline, watching the practice. She marvelled at Emma's graceful and agile movements. Her position of centre allowed her to cover most of the field and she seemed to be everywhere, dodging her opponent and never missing a catch. Maha was shooting well and most of her shots went through the ring. Every time Maha scored, Talia cheered loudly and was rewarded with a huge grin from Maha.

Simon, however, was feeling out of place on the netball court. He could catch any ball that was remotely near him but he was constantly bumping into other players. Ms Nixon kept blowing her whistle emphatically every few minutes.

"No contact allowed in netball, mister!" she yelled at him.

But Ms Nixon knew that as soon as he mastered the no-contact rule and stopped running with the ball like a rugby player, he would be a great asset to the team.

As Ms Nixon blew the final whistle, Talia ran up to her to find out about her duties. Ms Nixon had to rack her brains for a few moments. She knew that it was vital to make Talia feel important and part of the team.

"Well, you have to make a list of all the students that attend each practice and match. You are also responsible for bringing and collecting the balls and netball bibs for every practice and match."

Talia looked very serious and nodded. Then Ms Nixon had a brainwave. She had heard about Talia's artistic ability from the art teacher, "And I want you to decorate the netball bibs with the school name and crest."

Talia was delighted. Never before had a teacher given her such an important task. She gathered the bibs from the players and quickly pulled a piece of paper and pen from among the jumble in her bag and, with an air of importance, asked the players to write down their names.

Mrs Leveson sat in her Lexus, anxiously waiting for her daughter. Ever since Talia had called her to say that she was playing netball, she had felt extremely concerned. When Talia was younger, Mrs Leveson had spent hours patiently and sometimes not so patiently throwing a ball to Talia in the backyard while barking instructions but at the last moment the ball would slip through her fingers. Mrs Leveson had continued in vain until one day Talia picked up the ball, slammed it to the ground and shouted, "No more!" and stormed off.

The door of the car swung open and Talia announced proudly, "I'm the manager of the team!"

Her mother, stunned for a moment, stared at her and was greeted by a beaming smile. And before she could respond, Talia added, "I need art supplies to decorate the bibs."

Her mum was just about to ask about her homework but the rare look of bliss on her daughter's face kept her silent and she drove directly to the art shop.

When they arrived home, Talia did not even switch on the television but went straight to the computer and began to type the names of the children who had attended the practice. She took great care with each letter as she knew that she still sometimes confused 'b' and 'd' and that the order of the letters often got jumbled. Her mum stood at the doorway, watching her with amazement. She had never seen her sitting and concentrating at the computer for any period of time. But what was even more astonishing was that Talia was wearing her glasses. No amount of cajoling and bribery from her mother could entice her to wear the glasses and they had remained untouched in the case until now. Talia checked and rechecked the list and only then did she print it out and place it in a file before carefully storing it in her bag.

Talia settled herself at the large wooden table and carefully sorted her paints. While letters and numbers always seemed to evaporate, colours and pictures were forever emblazoned on her brain. She carefully studied the school emblem on her blazer. At the centre stood the red waratah, surrounded by the kookaburra, the platypus and the bright blue groper. She remembered being told that they were all symbols of New South Wales. Underneath were the large letters in gold, 'D.E.P.S'.

"Darlinghurst East Public School," she whispered to herself. She dipped her brush in the red, diluted it with a touch of white to make it pink and began to paint. Soon she was so completely engrossed in the world of colours that she didn't even hear her mum calling her for dinner two hours later.

Tuesday Morning:
1 March 2011

The students were talking excitedly among themselves when Mr Zulman entered the classroom. Emma, Simon and Maha had been chosen to play in the 'A' netball team and next to Talia's name, Ms Nixon had printed 'MANAGER' in bold letters.

Mr Zulman wrote on the board, 'Freedom'. He then stepped back and looked at it for a moment, deep in thought and began to talk:

"The story of Passover can be seen as the struggle for freedom. Passover is the Jewish festival, which celebrates freedom. Freedom allows us to do what we want as long as we don't hurt anyone else. In Australia, the laws of our country ensure that we are free and that everyone is equal. We have the freedom to say what we want and express our views as long they are not harmful to another. We have the freedom to go wherever we desire without anyone restricting our movement. We also have the freedom to be in contact with a person or people of our choice, just as you four have chosen to be friends despite coming from different backgrounds."

Talia stopped listening while the words of Mr Zulman rolled around and echoed in her head: "Freedom! Every person equal, move freely, speak freely." She remembered clearly that day just two weeks before her family had left South Africa for Australia. Her heart was already heavy with the impending loss of her beloved nanny Gladys because she had wanted to spend every minute with her. Gladys was sitting on a blanket in the shade of the drooping branches of the willow tree at the bottom of the garden, polishing the silver. She started walking towards Gladys. The newly mown grass was like a soft carpet under her bare feet and the African gardener was trimming the edges of the garden beds, dead straight, just as her mother liked them. She stretched out next to Gladys. She had looked at her and realised that she knew nothing about her other than that she appeared every morning and that she had always loved and looked after her.

"Where do you live, Gladys?"

Gladys had looked up from her polishing with surprise. "Why do you want to know, Nyenyane?"

"I want to know about your life," she had said with determination.

Gladys had remained silent for a few minutes. She then

POL
ISH

replied, "I live in a place called Soweto where still only black people live. No whites."

She mumbled softly to herself, "A bit better now after apartheid, at least I have electricity."

"What is apartheid? And why is it a little better now?"

"You don't need to know, Nyenyane."

"I am leaving soon. I want to know. I need to know!" she had insisted.

Gladys had sighed.

"Until 1991, the South African government made us live under apartheid. I will tell you what my life was like and then you will understand apartheid." She stopped for a moment and said under her breath, "Your mother won't be happy with me."

She continued, "At that time, black people were forced to live in separate areas, away from the white people. I would wake up at four o'clock on a winter morning and light a candle. We had no electricity. I would throw a blanket over my shoulders to try to keep warm. My fingers were so frozen that I used to struggle to drag the heavy pot of water onto the primus stove to heat some water to have a quick wash. My husband was not there to help me and I did not see him for a year at a time. He had to work 100 kilometres away in a gold mine. It was still dark when I would walk to the bus station. The smoke all around me from the chimneys of the tin shanties would make me cough and I walked quickly trying not to fall in the potholes in the dirt roads; there were no tarred roads like in your suburb. There were no bus shelters for the blacks and the wind would bite us. Then I would hear the boom-boom of the old busses arriving. All the new ones were for the whites only. I had to push my way onto the bus and often we would hear the shouting of the policemen when they jumped out of their vans. I always had to keep my 'pass' with me, which was a piece of paper that said I could work, ready to show them. But some people didn't and they would start running in all directions. The police had these big sticks and knocked people to the ground and threw them into the back of police vans. When my bus finally stopped in the suburb where only the whites lived, it was like coming to a new world. I was often late, so I'd have to run past the big houses with the high walls and the dogs would bark at me. As I opened the gate to your house, madam would be waiting for me, hands on hips—you know how your mother hates anyone to be late—and I would say, 'Sorry madam'. You just can't explain to anyone who lives in a palace what it is like to live in a slum. I don't like to tell you such stories, Nyenyane."

Talia was brought back to the present by the scrape of Mr Zulman's chair as he got up and started to pace up and down the room. Mr Zulman was looking at Maha with the expectation that she would speak, knowing that she had lived in a war-torn country. But today Maha did not want to talk about that part of her life. She was feeling so happy that she did not want to revisit those dark memories. Instead she said, "I love living in Sydney because here we are free. I go to mosque or not. I decide. My family, we walk in the street; we go to parks. We are never scared. No one tells me what I can or can't say and now I choose to speak no more."

She finished with a flourish and a self-satisfied smile lit up her face.

Mr Zulman looked at Maha with interest. He was happy to see that the timid, silent girl had almost disappeared and that she was becoming bolder by the week.

"Quite correct," responded Mr Zulman. "You have the freedom to remain silent."

Simon interceded with an air of self-importance: "My mum is a lawyer. She says everyone is innocent until proven guilty, which I think means that you can't just throw someone in jail without a fair trial and take away his freedom."

"Good point, Simon. In Australia we live in a democracy where the laws of this country protect the freedom of its citizens," added Mr Zulman.

Emma always felt at a bit of a loss during these discussions as she had lived her entire life in Sydney and had never even contemplated the idea of freedom; she had simply taken it for granted.

Talia heard Mr Zulman call her name and saw that he was now looking at her waiting for her to speak. She did not want to share Gladys' story. The bell rang and she breathed a sigh of relief. *Saved by the bell,* she thought to herself.

Tuesday Afternoon

It was the first netball match of the season and the players gathered on the court. The team, like young fillies, paced back and forth. Talia handed each player a bib and as she was doing so, Ms Nixon stared at them incredulously. She could not believe that this uncoordinated girl on the netball court had hand-painted each one so beautifully. She admired the vibrant, subtle shading of reds and blues. Ms Nixon walked over to Talia, patted her on the back and said, "Excellent job, Talia, almost a pity to let them wear them!" Talia, unaccustomed to praise, just smiled delightedly.

As the teams took their positions, Talia settled herself on the sideline. A tall blonde woman who was dressed in shorts, a singlet and flip-flops came strolling towards her and even before she could identify herself, Talia recognised her as Emma's mum. The long, easy stride, the blue eyes and the smile that curled up at the corners were identical. She also had that same easy, friendly manner.

"You must be Talia, the team manager. I'm Kerri, Emma's

mum," she said and sat down on the ground cross-legged next to Talia.

Talia thought wryly to herself that her mum would never sit on the ground as she always said that her linen pants creased so easily.

The players took up their positions in readiness for the start of the match. Emma had been given her usual position as centre and stood poised with the ball in her hands, waiting for the whistle to start play. Maha was goal shooter and was standing, anxiously looking around while Simon, who had been put in the position of goal defence, was in a semi-crouched stance as if preparing for a rugby scrum. A few of the girls in the other team looked at him and giggled. The whistle blew and the match began with Emma throwing a strong, straight ball into the hands of her wing attack. Within seconds Maha had broken free of her defender and had the ball in her hands and was aiming to shoot. Talia noted with concern Maha's trembling hand and the ball bypassed the ring.

"You can do it!" she shouted encouragingly from the sideline.

Maha gave her a grateful half-smile, disappointed with herself for having missed the opportunity for a goal for her team. As the game progressed, Talia became more and more mesmerised by Emma's athletic figure and ball skills.

She never dropped a ball and her throws were direct and powerful. But Talia was concerned about her other two friends who were not performing as well. The flash of red hair was everywhere, accompanied by the constant shrill blowing of the whistles by the umpires as Simon, in his eagerness, kept crossing over the line and bumping into his opponents. Maha too had not settled into the match. Time and time again Emma passed the ball to Maha but in her nervousness, she aimed and shot too quickly. She had not yet scored. Talia could identify with Maha. Anxiety had been her constant companion for as long as she could remember. Then the realisation dawned on her that she no longer had that tight knot of nervousness at the pit of her stomach and she was flooded with happiness mingled with relief.

Mrs Beaumont sensed Talia's concern with the team and reassured her, "Don't worry, Talia, they are still learning. They'll come good!"

The whistle sounded for half-time and the team gathered around Ms Nixon. Talia started handing out the glasses of chilled water and orange quarters. The players gulped down the water gratefully and then sucked noisily on the oranges while Ms Nixon spoke to them.

"Three feet from your opponent," she heard Ms Nixon remind Simon.

Talia noticed that Maha was standing apart from the team, eyes downcast, slowly sipping her water. Talia joined her. “Breathe deeply and concentrate,” she whispered to Maha. Talia had heard those words time and time again over the years from her mother and she could not quite believe that she was repeating them to her friend. Maha looked at her gratefully but her face remained solemn.

The teams took up their positions in readiness for the second half. The centre for the other team held the ball and Emma positioned herself on the line in a defensive position in front of the wing attack. The first ball was thrown and Emma stretched out and intercepted the throw and within seconds the ball was again in the hands of Maha. Talia held her breath. She saw Maha steadying herself, taking aim and shooting. And lo and behold, she scored her first goal of the match. In her excitement, Talia ran onto the court and hugged Maha, who laughed happily.

“Off the court, Talia!” shouted Ms Nixon but without her usual volume, clearly relieved that Maha had scored.

Simon also seemed to settle into the match and only intermittently collided with his opponent when his eagerness got the better of him. When the final whistle sounded, Darlinghurst East had won by just two goals, with Maha scoring most of the goals. The team were delighted with their first game of the season and Ms

Nixon congratulated each team member on their effort and sportsmanship. Talia gathered the bibs from the players, feeling very much part of the team's victory.

Simon picked up his school bag in readiness to make his way home. His elation was quickly turning into loneliness as he realised that he had no one with whom to share his victory. He saw Emma chatting animatedly with her mother as they began to walk towards their car. Mrs Beaumont had thrown her arm over Emma's shoulder, which only added to his feeling of isolation. Simon sat on the short bus ride home revisiting all the play of the match and concluded that he had definitely contributed to the victory, feeling quite self-satisfied. But when he stepped off the bus, lonesomeness again enveloped him.

Mr Naidoo saw him sauntering by in his sports gear and called out, "Did you just have a match, Simon?"

"Yes, we won," he responded without much enthusiasm.

Fearing the solitude of home, he walked into the shop and sat down on the stool behind the counter. His face was still bright red. Mr Naidoo opened the fridge and pulled out a can of creaming soda, which he knew was Simon's favourite and handed it to him saying, "Free for you today to celebrate your victory!"

Simon thanked him, gulped it down and left. He wanted to chat but only with his mum or dad.

As he entered the unit, he heard the phone ring and was glad to hear his mother's voice. Now he could tell her about the match.

But before he could begin, she said, "Tell me all about it when I get home but I may be late."

Simon recognised that brisk tone of his mum when she was very busy and knew that there was no point in trying to continue the conversation.

"Fine, see you later," he said and hung up.

He kicked the chair in anger. He wondered bitterly to himself why they had such a large apartment when there was nobody to fill it. He opened the freezer, took out a frozen macaroni and cheese and put it in the microwave. Once his meal was warmed, he sat on the couch nibbling his food without much appetite and began listlessly flicking the channels.

When it was already dark, the idea suddenly occurred to him to call his dad and tell him all about the match. He excitedly dialled the eight-digit number that he had memorised and waited. It was only when he heard the drowsy voice of his father did he remember that it was the middle of the night in Los Angeles.

"Is everything OK?" he heard the concerned voice of his father.

"Sorry, I forgot the time," he mumbled. "Wanted to tell you about my netball match," his voice trailing off.

"You play netball?" asked his father incredulously, now wide awake.

Simon did not want to explain why he had chosen netball and neither did he now have any desire to describe the match.

"Go back to sleep, Dad. We'll speak on the weekend. Sorry for waking you," he muttered and quickly put down the phone.

He had never felt more alone and by the time his mother returned home much later in the evening, Simon was fast asleep.

Tuesday Morning:
8 March 2011

Mr Zulman stood staring out the window, waiting for his students to arrive. The weather had turned overnight, the skies were dark and the rain was pouring down outside.

Perfect atmosphere for describing the plagues, he thought to himself as the students came rushing into the room out of the rain.

"Today we are going to talk about the ten plagues in Egypt. We know that Moses, together with his brother Aaron, was sent by God to free the slaves. Moses and Aaron represent those that continue to fight to free the oppressed, whereas Pharaoh represents those that stand stubbornly like an immovable barrier obstructing the path to freedom. Sometimes the barrier is within ourselves and we have to fight to set ourselves free."

Mr Zulman saw Maha looking at him quizzically and he realised that again he had got caught up in his own words, not taking Maha into account.

"What I am trying to say," he began with an apologetic tone, "is that there are people or rulers of countries like Pharaoh who prevent people from living in freedom."

Maha nodded as if she understood.

Mr Zulman continued, "What I am also saying is that sometimes we have feelings like fear or doubt within us and that we have to work towards being free to be ourselves."

Maha looked at Mr Zulman. "I understand," she said simply, "like at the first netball match when I was so nervous. I couldn't shoot. Then Talia helped me…how do you say… be sure of myself!"

"Exactly," said Mr Zulman. "Now let's continue with the struggle for freedom."

He continued:

"Time and time again, Pharaoh changed his mind and refused to allow the slaves to leave Egypt. One day, God commanded Moses to take Pharaoh down to the river. Moses told Aaron to take a rod and strike the water. When he did so, all the water turned to blood. For seven days the Egyptians had no water to drink and Moses returned to Pharaoh, warning him that if he refused to free the slaves, the land would be over-run with frogs. Again Pharaoh refused, so Aaron lifted his rod over the river, canals and pools, and slimy frogs came up and covered the land of Egypt. The frogs filled every space. Slippery frogs hopped around the houses, into their beds, onto the people and even invaded their ovens and the troughs where they kneaded the dough. The Egyptians were suffering and Pharaoh called Moses and told him that he would free the slaves if Moses got rid of the frogs. However, when Moses did so, Pharaoh changed his mind. So God commanded Moses to tell Aaron to strike the ground and the land was covered with lice. Now, if you have ever experienced head lice, you will know that you can't stop scratching. Just imagine having lice not just crawling in your hair but covering your entire body."

The children scratched their heads uncomfortably as they thought of the lice.

"Pharaoh agreed to free the slaves if Moses removed the lice. But again, once it had been done, he changed his mind. The cycle continued. During each plague, Pharaoh would agree to free the Israelites but when Moses stopped the plague, Pharaoh would change his mind. Moses brought down frightening plagues, like wild beasts that roamed the land, followed by disease of their cattle and horrid boils that covered man and beast. Then the sky was alight with bolts of lightning and hail came thundering down, destroying everything including all the crops."

The children squirmed in their seats.

"The eighth plague was locusts, the ugliest and hugest

locusts that had ever or would ever be seen upon the earth and they were so numerous that they devoured everything that remained from the hail, until no green remained in Egypt. When Pharaoh changed his mind yet again, the land was plunged into darkness. The final plague, which was the most brutal, was the killing of the first born of the Egyptians."

Mr Zulman noted the look of horror that passed over his students' faces.

"With this terrible plague, there was a great cry of sorrow in the land and finally Pharaoh called Moses and ordered him to lead the slaves out of Egypt. At last, they would be free."

Mr Zulman stopped and stood there pensively for a moment before continuing to speak.

"This story can be seen as a relentless fight for freedom. Each new plague increases in intensity, teaching us that we too need to increase the intensity of our sometimes painful struggle until we are free. Even in our everyday lives, we have to continuously strive to overcome what holds us and others back."

"Mr Zulman..." began Emma slowly.

Mr Zulman turned to her with a tinge of surprise as she was definitely not the most vocal of this group.

"Yes, Emma," and he looked at her encouragingly.

"Well, you know how I told the story of the stolen generation."

She looked at Maha and added, "About the Aboriginal children that were taken from their mothers and fathers, not that long ago." Everyone waited for her to continue.

"Well, about three years ago, I woke up ready to go to school and my mother said that it was a very important day and that we were going into the city. I was excited as we were going to catch a train there. We walked to Martin Place where there were these huge screens. The prime minister came on the screen and apologised on behalf of all Australians to those people who had been stolen as children. I remember thinking that it was a bit strange that there were people around me crying while there were other people rushing to work that only glanced at the screen. I must admit, I was mostly happy to be missing school."

Emma thought for a moment and continued, "Afterwards we went for hot chocolate at the David Jones store in the city and my mum said that the Aborigines had fought for a very long time for this day."

Mr Zulman nodded in agreement.

As they left the classroom, Emma, feeling the need for a space that was theirs alone, turned to the others and said, "Let's go onto the rooftop. I'll meet you guys there. Just going to get my ball."

Before Maha and Talia started making their way up the winding stairs, Simon dipped into Maha's lunch box, took out a pitta filled with tabouli and left a packet of chips and a muesli bar in its place. He ran off to join the boys on the soccer field, which his father had insisted upon after hearing that he was playing netball. The girls sat eating their morning tea and enjoying the soft sea breeze while Emma threw the ball against the wall, catching it at all angles. Maha stood up, held out her hands and called out to Emma, "To me!" and they threw the ball to each other while Talia watched them contentedly until the bell rang.

Tuesday Afternoon

The students sat waiting impatiently for the final bell. The four friends walked towards the netball court nervously, discussing the game ahead of them. They had been victorious in all their matches up to now but today they were playing Lindfield Park School, which had been the grand-final winners for the previous five years.

"I've heard that they train three times a week and we only train once," said Emma to Maha with concern in her voice. As soon as they arrived at the netball court, Emma called to her teammates and organised them into a circle with herself at the centre and began throwing the ball back and forth. Talia thought to herself that Emma was definitely queen of the netball court and that the team responded well to her leadership, which was never bossy and somehow just right. When Ms Nixon arrived, they were warming up by running around the court with Emma in front. Talia had the bibs neatly folded over her arm, which always surprised her mates as they knew Talia to be extremely untidy in the classroom. She handed them out and settled herself on the ground next to Mrs Beaumont as she did for every match. Talia always felt at ease and completely accepted in Mrs Beaumont's company but wished that it was her mother beside her.

Play began and Emma dominated the court as usual. Maha had achieved a rhythm and almost all her shots now went into the ring. Every time she scored for her team, Talia cheered loudly and Maha smiled broadly in response. Simon's skills had also improved immeasurably and he was proving to be an invaluable defence player. But today he was overeager and kept bumping into his opponent. When he was penalised for the third time by the umpires for making contact, he slammed the ball down in frustration. By the time Ms Nixon blew the whistle for half-time, the Lindfield Park team were in the lead by three goals and not even looking tired. Talia started handing out the oranges. She heard the angry voice of Ms Nixon behind her, "Over here, Simon—now!"

The team tried to avert their eyes but took surreptitious glances in their direction. An angry Ms Nixon was a terrifying sight and to have her looming over Simon was even scarier. Even though she was talking softly, her gruff voice carried and the team could hear words such as, "Won't tolerate bad sportsmanship…last chance…out on your ear!" and then she stormed off. Simon hung his head in shame and his face looked as if it was on fire. His three friends immediately gathered around him and spoke to him soothingly. "You're new to the game, defence is a difficult position," advised Emma.

"Yeah," echoed Talia, "must be really difficult."

"You try hard!" encouraged Maha.

The whistle blew and the team took up their positions in readiness for the second half.

At the start of the second half, Simon was downcast and did not play with his usual exuberance. He made a concerted effort not to make contact with his opponent. Every time he intercepted a ball, Emma shouted encouragement, "Well done, Simon!" and Talia and Mrs Beaumont cheered from the sideline. But before long, he was absorbed in the game and when he did make contact with his opponent, he would pick up the ball and politely hand it to her with a half-smile at Ms Nixon. She acknowledged his good behaviour with a nod of her head. When the final whistle blew, the match had ended with a draw and the team were delighted. Talia collected the bibs and ball. Ms Nixon, who was quick to anger and equally quick to forgive, congratulated the team and said to Simon in earshot of the team, "You defended well in the second half and exhibited good sportsmanship!" and he knew that all was forgiven.

The four friends started walking towards the gate

together with Mrs Beaumont. They heard her asking Emma, "How about takeaway pizza while watching a DVD tonight?"

"Sounds good," Emma responded casually.

The other three looked on enviously. Talia's mother never bought takeaway food as she said that it increased Talia's hyperactivity. Talia also liked the idea of not always sitting around a table, which her mother always insisted upon. Takeaway food was only too familiar to Simon but he invariably ate it alone and would have loved some company for once. Pizza was still foreign to Maha as she had only tasted it once when Simon had brought a cold slice to school and she had liked it immediately. Her parents, like Talia's, also insisted upon the family eating at a table every night. In Iraq, the table had once been a carved antique cedar one and now it was a scrubbed, stained pine table that they had picked up on the side of the road on council pick-up day. Her mother would sometimes sigh as she looked at the table but Maha didn't care as she enjoyed the time she spent with her parents sitting around it chatting.

Tuesday Morning:
15 March 2011

Mr Zulman opened the door and was startled as the room was plunged into darkness.

"Beware everyone! You have entered Egypt!" screamed Talia at the top of her lungs.

He waited for a few seconds for his eyes to adjust to the darkness. The windows had been covered in black fabric. Sounds of booming thunder and pounding rain blasted out from a CD player. *These must all be Talia's ideas,* he thought to himself.

He looked at the cups of red cordial. "Blood!" shouted Simon, and Mr Zulman suspected from the way they were running about wildly that they had already drunk a fair bit of it. Mr Zulman tentatively took a few steps as the floor was splattered in polystyrene hail. Simon was covered in green fabric and was hopping around, pretending to be a frog. Emma, who had chosen to be a wild beast, was dressed in a leopard design leotard with horns attached to her forehead and was crawling around snarling at everyone. Talia was dressed as a locust. She wore a brown swimsuit and every bit of visible skin was dotted with lime green and dirty-brown paint. Twisted pipe cleaners were attached to the top of her head and she ran around with her mouth open, pretending to eat everything in sight.

Only Maha was slightly subdued. She had agreed to be Moses and had attached a white cottonwool beard to her chin. She walked around saying, “Let my people go!” The others kept prompting her, “Louder, Maha, louder!” Mr Zulman was aware of her discomfort with the darkness and as soon as he could calm the children down, he removed the black fabric from the windows and immediately noted Maha’s relief.

“I think it is time to leave plague-infested Egypt!” he suggested but they were too excited to stop and continued in their roles until the bell rang.

Tuesday Afternoon

Maha and Emma walked out of the school gates together. Maha had asked Emma to go shopping with her the previous day and Emma had readily agreed. Maha had grown out of all her clothes. Her dresses were becoming so tight that she had to hold her breath while her mother struggled to do up the zip. Her toes were red and inflamed from sitting curled up in her shoes. She had spotted a store where she was sure that she could get cheap second-hand clothes. She knew that it would be humiliating for her mother to go into such a store, as their clothes in Iraq had always been handmade with the best fabrics until her father was unable to work anymore. So she had convinced her mum to let her go to the shop with her friend.

The two girls arrived and stood outside the store. Emma read the sign: "St Vincent de Paul."

"Wow, it's a Vinnies shop!" she said with surprise.

Emma knew that her mother had always donated their old furniture to a Vinnies but she had never been into any of their shops. She felt Maha's eyes on her.

"What are we waiting for? Let's shop!" Emma said with feigned enthusiasm.

The rusty bell above them rang as they entered, alerting the attendant. A musty smell hung in the air and tickled their noses and Maha sneezed three times in a row.

"What can I do for you, young ladies?" a kindly old, grey-haired lady said in greeting. Emma looked at her friend who seemed to have been struck dumb in between sneezes as she stood staring at the racks of old clothing and the piles of furniture at the rear of the shop.

"We are looking for shoes and clothes for my friend," responded Emma with a certainty that she did not feel.

"We have some lovely, pretty clothes but no shoes unfortunately. Follow me."

The girls walked behind her obediently. She stopped in front of the children's clothing.

"Pick out whatever you want," encouraged the woman.

Maha didn't move.

I'll pretend that I am taking charge like on the netball court, thought Emma.

It was hard for Emma as she had only ever bought new clothes but she knew that it would have even been harder for Maha to wear second-hand clothes. She began to rustle through the clothing. She chose a floral blue skirt and found a matching ruffled top. Maha's face brightened and

Emma kept piling clothes into Maha's arms until she was laden with a colourful array of clothing.

"No charge for those," said the woman cheerfully.

Maha shook her head and carefully pulled out a twenty-dollar note that her mum had given her.

The woman smiled, "Give me $10 and let's call it even!"

The girls happily left the store with Maha holding her bulky package.

Tuesday Morning: 22 March 2011

Mr Zulman walked into the classroom at the same time as the students. They immediately noticed that he was wearing flip-flops.

"Before you all ask, I forgot my shoes. I went for a swim this morning and I didn't have time to go home to fetch them," he explained with a grin that made Talia's heart melt. The four students could not stop staring at his enormous feet.

"If you can take your eyes off my feet for just a minute, we can continue with the story of the slaves," he said with a laugh.

The children reluctantly began to pay attention, except for Talia, who continued to stare and thought to herself that she must find a way to watch him in the surf.

"When the Israelites heard that they were to be set free, they hurriedly packed their few belongings," began Mr Zulman. "They did not have time to let their bread rise for the journey and so took unrisen or 'unleavened bread', as it is known, with them. That very same night, the Israelites followed Moses out of the land of Egypt into the wilderness.

God led the people with a huge cloud by day, which always hovered over them, and a pillar of bright fire by night. The Israelites travelled to the Red Sea and as they stood before this vast expanse of water, Pharaoh changed his mind. He ordered his captains to take six hundred chariots and pursue the slaves. The slaves stood trapped between the huge waves of the Red Sea that rolled before them and the soldiers in their chariots galloping towards them from behind. They had nowhere to go."

Mr Zulman paused for a moment.

"Would they drown in the waves of the Red Sea or would the soldiers force them to return to slavery?"

The children sat on the edge of their chairs, waiting for Mr Zulman to continue. He let the question hang in the air for a few seconds before continuing.

"The slaves cried out to God in despair. God commanded Moses to lift up his rod and the sea split before them. Imagine yourself standing on the edge of Bondi Beach, when the sea suddenly splits open and there is a dry path before you. The slaves grabbed their belongings and rushed forward, desperately trying to escape the soldiers. And as the soldiers drew nearer and were about to reach them, the sea closed over the oppressors and the slaves escaped. The slaves were finally liberated."

The children let out a sigh of relief.

Tuesday Afternoon

As the netball season progressed, Ms Nixon's expectations grew and she pushed them harder and harder each week. The team maintained their second place behind Lindfield Park School. Talia attended all the practices although she was not really needed. That afternoon, she walked slowly down towards the netball court as the others ran ahead, afraid to keep Ms Nixon waiting. She breathed a sigh of relief that she was not a player in the team when she saw the formidable figure of Ms Nixon in her usual bright red tracksuit. Ms Nixon stood hands on hips, whistle hanging from her neck, waiting impatiently for the arrival of the team. Before they even had a chance to put down their bags, she roared at the players, "Start running around the field, we don't have all day. Now!"

Talia sat down and took the list of players from a plastic sleeve in her folder and began to meticulously mark off the names of those present. She then carefully returned the sheet to the plastic sleeve. It annoyed her mother at how neatly she kept the list amidst a school bag strewn with crumpled papers that was getting messier as the term progressed. The team were now running around in a circle, throwing the ball to each other. Talia noticed that Maha was moving with some discomfort and wondered if she had somehow injured herself. Maha was indeed in agony as she had outgrown her sports shoes as well now, so that her toes hit the front of them every time she ran. She had to squeeze her feet into the shoes, wincing with pain as her toes and heels had become raw and swollen. She did not tell her mother as she knew that money was tight and that they struggled to buy the basic household necessities, let alone luxury goods like sports shoes.

Ms Nixon divided them into two teams and they began to play a game against each other. Ms Nixon's whistle was permanently perched between her lips and the piercing sound was followed by a constant stream of instructions. When the practice ended, the team gratefully left the court. Even Emma was covered in sweat, although Ms Nixon had not corrected her even once. Simon's face was the colour of beetroot and he poured a bottle of water over his head in an effort to cool down. Maha sank to the ground and slowly pulled off her shoes and Talia saw her red inflamed toes.

After netball practice, Talia climbed into her mother's car and announced, "I need new sports shoes."

Her mother looked at her with surprise, "But Talia, you never play sport!"

"I am the manager and need running shoes and we have to buy them today!"

The grey clouds looked menacing but her mother knew that when Talia made up her mind about something, there would be no dissuading her.

Rather like myself, she thought with a hint of pride as she headed for Bondi Junction Shopping Centre. Talia sat in Athlete's Foot and was taking an extraordinary amount of time in making a choice. Talia was trying to decide which shoes would be most suitable for Maha. In her haste, she had forgotten to look at the size of Maha's feet. The salesman had brought out various styles of sports shoes which Talia had insisted upon and he was now waiting for her to choose.

"Talia, we are going to be caught in the hail storm. Decide now or I will decide for you!" threatened her mother.

Talia pointed to a pair of Nikes and added, "But one size bigger."

Just in case, she thought to herself.

The salesman and her mother stared at her in astonishment. Talia had spent close to an hour finding the correct fit. In normal circumstances, her mother would have argued with her but her desire to get home before the storm hit was greater, so she just paid and walked hurriedly to the car. They were pulling into their garage when the storm broke. Her mother gave into her annoyance: "I would have been furious if my car had been hail damaged for a pair of shoes one size too big!"

Tuesday Morning: 29 March 2011

The friends were taking their time walking to the Jewish Scripture class. Talia had been trying to decide the whole week what was the best way to give the shoes to Maha without embarrassing her. She now had the new shoes in a box under her arm, "Can you believe it..." she began. "My stupid mother made me buy these sports shoes. I'm the manager. What on earth am I going to do with them? Do me a favour and take them off me, Maha." And before Maha could respond, Talia shoved the box into her hands and continued to walk quickly to class.

As the students entered the classroom, Mr Zulman came striding in behind them. They checked to see if he had remembered his shoes this time and were a little disappointed to discover that he had. He unrolled huge white sheets of paper and placed one on each desk and while he distributed the paints and coloured pencils, he began to speak:

"I have taken you on a journey with Moses and the

Israelites from slavery and pain to freedom and choice. At the same time, we too have journeyed and bravely shared our own pain and difficulties with each other. Just as the slaves emerged from darkness into the light, perhaps you too have moved forward into the light of understanding."

The children had become so used to Mr Zulman's barrage of words that they did not even bother to ask him to explain what he meant. Emma leant over to Maha and whispered, "I think he wants us to draw what we have learnt about ourselves from these classes."

Mr Zulman moved to the back of the classroom so as not to disturb his students with his presence but placed himself in a position to observe their art. He noticed that Emma was the first to start drawing and he smiled to himself remembering how she had sat staring at her blank sheet at the beginning of the term. Emma filled the page with the red sand of Central Australia and, in the centre, placed herself as a stick figure holding a netball. She surrounded herself with smiling little Aboriginal children with their hands outstretched, waiting to catch the ball. Mr Zulman thought to himself that it was as if she was peering into a crystal ball, seeing herself when she was grown up.

Mr Zulman glanced over at Simon's drawing. Simon was drawing himself on the netball court surrounded by his teammates. Mr Zulman saw him hesitate for a moment, pick up a pencil and then draw a tall, thin woman on the sideline. He hesitated again and drew a large man next to her but not quite touching. He drew their outstretched arms waving and cheering for him.

Mr Zulman looked over Maha's shoulder. He could recognise the sails of the Opera House and saw that she had selected the brightest blue colour to paint a cloudless Sydney sky.

She continued by painting a calm, silvery sea and a solid sailing boat. She drew four smiling children on the deck and a muscular man with strong hands that he recognised as himself at the helm.

Talia's page was ablaze with colour. At the centre of the page was a smiling woman with dark skin wearing a skirt of the brightest red and orange fabric, and dancing around her were four laughing children. There was a boy with bright-red hair, a girl with thick black braids, a girl with short blonde hair and a girl with a mop of wild curls and shining radiant eyes. Mr Zulman watched as she sat back and surveyed her work. Talia picked up her pencil and began to sketch next to the black woman a man with bulging muscles, damp hair and arms speckled with sea sand and he knew that he had been included within her circle.

Tuesday Afternoon

Maha was walking home after netball practice deep in thought. She had taken the shoes out of the box that Talia had given her and stuffed them into the bottom of her bag. She had played netball in her old shoes and with each step her toes throbbed. There was even a piercing pain in the arch of her foot. She knew that her parents would not let her keep the new shoes even though Talia had said that her mother had forced her to buy them. *I need them for the semi-finals and can't let my team down,* she argued with herself.

When she arrived home, she saw her mum staring out the window. The building was in the same street as the Belvoir Theatre and her parents would often stand melancholically staring out the window at the actors and the theatre-goers arriving before a play. Maha checked that the shoes were well hidden and joined her mother, who commented with disdain at how sloppily the people dressed. The vision flashed before her eyes from when she was a little girl, of her mother in a flowing silver, sequined dress as she joined her father in his navy striped suit on the way to the theatre in

Baghdad, leaving behind a waft of sweet-smelling perfume. Maha was startled out of her daydream with the thump of the bucket, mop and vacuum cleaner being dropped by the door. Her father silently joined them and greeted Maha with a kiss on the head and the three of them continued to watch the theatre-goers until it grew dark.

Friday Afternoon: 31 March 2011

The Friday of the semi-finals was an unusually scorching day for March. The team stood around Ms Nixon with a mixture of excitement and anxiety receiving their last minute pep talk while the Normanhurst team huddled around their coach. Their faces were plastered with sunscreen under their caps. Talia noticed that Maha was wearing the new sports shoes. Unbeknown to Talia, Maha had stuffed the front with newspaper as the shoes were too big. They felt strange but Maha had decided that it was preferable to her old ones. Ms Nixon blew the whistle for the start of play. Within the first minute, Maha scored the first goal of the match and from that moment, the Darlinghurst East team dominated. Both Talia and Mrs Beaumont agreed that the team had never played better. As usual, the darting, graceful figure of Emma was everywhere. Simon defended with vigour and only got penalised twice for contact, which was a record for him and there was almost a magical connection between Maha's hand and the ring. They established an early lead and by the end of the match, they had trounced Normanhurst by twenty goals. Ms Nixon could barely hide her delight and congratulated the team in her cryptic way, "Good play and good sportsmanship," she said.

Emma ran breathlessly up to her mum and said, "Mum, can I take my friends to McDonalds to celebrate?"

"Of course," she responded and Emma eagerly went to invite her friends.

Simon called his mother on his mobile and left a message. Talia ran over to her mother's car and announced that she was celebrating with the team and would be getting a lift home, not even waiting for permission or to hear the usual instructions as to what she could or could not eat. Even Maha was happy to go as her parents knew about the game and expected her to be home later than usual.

The four friends, together with Mrs Beaumont, started walking towards McDonalds, which was a couple of blocks away from the school. When they arrived, Emma ordered a Happy Meal with extra large chips. Simon and Talia ordered the same while Maha, overwhelmed with the choice and not sure what she was permitted to eat due to Muslim Halal laws, hesitantly chose the fish burger. Talia knew that her mother would have disapproved of her choice but did not care and was savouring every morsel of her meal. They all sat munching away happily while excitedly discussing the match. Simon, with a full mouth, described his every move.

"Did you see how the ball bounced off the edge of the post and I jumped in front of the goal shooter and caught it?" he asked his friends eagerly.

"Sure did! Excellent move," responded Emma. "And Maha, I don't think you missed a single shot!"

Mrs Beaumont listened with pride as Emma praised everyone else without mentioning her own splendid play.

When Talia started describing Emma's moves, she modestly diverted their attention to someone else.

The others were finishing their meal with a soft-serve ice-cream when Maha took leave of them. As soon as she was out of sight, she took off the sports shoes, carefully placed them at the bottom of her bag, stepped back into her school shoes and walked home happily.

Tuesday Morning:
5 April 2011

Mr Zulman was engrossed in his reading when the students arrived. He slowly unfurled his massive frame from the chair.

"We have spoken in the last few weeks of oppression and freedom. In the Jewish calendar, the festival of Passover is the festival of freedom. People come together on the night of Passover at what is called a 'Seder', which simply means 'order', as we retell the story of leaving Egypt as it unfolded. We recount the story with the feeling that we ourselves are being saved from slavery. At the centre of the table is placed what is called a 'Seder Plate'."

"We have a silver one at home," remarked Talia.

"Jewish people have all different kinds of plates but the foods that we put on them are the most important part," replied Mr Zulman.

"The various foods that are placed on the special Seder Plate help us to remember the different parts of the story that I have been telling you about throughout these classes. First is the 'matzah', which is the Hebrew word for unleavened, flat bread, because as we know, when the slaves fled from Pharaoh, they did not have time to let the bread rise. Then there is the 'charoset', the Hebrew word for a mixture of apples, nuts and cinnamon, which represents the bricks that the slaves had to make by hand. On the plate are bitter herbs such as horseradish to represent the harsh times in captivity. There is parsley, which is dipped in salt water to remember the tears of the oppressed. We also have a boiled egg, which is a sign of mourning for all the sad times in history and finally a bone to remember the sacrifice, which was the ancient way of praying, that the people made to give thanks to God for saving them."

Mr Zulman looked around at the children. Everyone looked bored and Talia was shuffling in her seat even more than usual. He felt a little disappointed that his presentation had not interested them. Trying to regain their attention, he suggested, "Perhaps we could have our own mock Seder demonstration."

Immediately Talia's face lit up and she interrupted excitedly, "Mr Zulman, I have a better idea. Why don't we have it at my house? We have a big Seder every year and so we have all the stuff for the demonstration."

"Well," began Mr Zulman, rubbing his fingers over the stubble on his chin, "we would not want to inconvenience your family." But before he could continue, Talia whipped out her mobile phone and began dialling her mother's number. Within a minute, she turned to the others. "All arranged for next week!" she announced importantly.

Mr Zulman was slightly taken aback by the speediness of the arrangement.

"Um, we will have to get signed permission forms from each parent. As there are only four of you, I will write out permission forms now."

Each child took a permission form and they started discussing the outing animatedly.

"What should we wear?" asked Emma.

"Party clothes," responded Talia.

Only Maha remained silent. She had still not told her parents that she was attending a class on the Jewish religion and was wondering how to get one of her parents to sign the permission form.

Tuesday Afternoon

As soon as Talia arrived home, she walked straight into the dining room to begin laying the table for their Seder. Her heart sank. Her mother had already taken out their crystal glasses and the ice white Villeroy and Boch dinner service, which sat next to a pile of starched fabric serviettes. She knew that her friends would be very uncomfortable in such a posh setting. She heard her mother's voice behind her, "Shall we start setting up?" Her mother asked, only to see that Talia looked completely deflated.

"What's the matter?" she asked concernedly.

"I kind of had my own ideas," she began hesitantly and handed her mother a diagram. Her mother noted with annoyance that the illustration was on the back of a maths sheet but for once she didn't criticise and conceded to her daughter.

"Well," as she looked at the diagram, "plastic plates and glasses, red paper serviettes and multi-coloured roses it is. I think we had better keep the silver Seder plate though, don't you think?"

"Sure," agreed Talia happily with a smile and they began to set the table together.

*

Maha was walking slowly home from school. She desperately wanted to go to the Seder at Talia's house. She calculatedly thought that her mum would be her best bet as she still had very limited English and might not ask too many questions or be able to work out the activity. Maha stood for a moment in front of their building. The building today looked even more dismal than usual except for the fluorescent coloured graffiti that was newly strewn across the front walls. Maha began to make her way carefully around the broken beer bottles lying in the foyer and she remembered how they had been woken in the middle of the previous night by the sound of shattering glass. Her mother was waiting for her when she entered the apartment. Maha plastered a smile on her face and, taking advantage of the absence of her father, told her mum that she was going on a school outing and needed her signature. She shoved a pen into her mother's hand. Mrs Hassan glanced at the notice and signed. Almost before Mrs Hassan had finished signing, Maha quickly grabbed it and put it into her bag.

"Shall we go to the shops?" she asked, successfully diverting attention from the notice.

*

At the same time, Simon was procrastinating on his way home. He kicked a few stones disconsolately. There was always this empty void that faced him on his return home from school. He waved to Mr Naidoo but was not in the mood to chat and continued ambling along. As he was taking the key from around his neck, he was enveloped with the aroma of fresh cooking. *Must be next door,* he thought bitterly to himself. He opened the door and there was his mum in an apron busily stirring what looked like a chocolate mixture in a huge bowl.

"Mum, what are you doing home so early?" he asked with a mixture of surprise and delight.

"I've come home to make choc-chip biscuits for my favourite son," she laughed. "Actually, I just pulled off a huge deal and decided to spend the remainder of the day with you. The leg of lamb and potatoes are already in the oven!"

Simon pulled out the permission form from his bag, settled himself happily on the stool in the kitchen and began to lick the bowl contentedly.

He started telling his mum about the Seder, "Passover is the festival of freedom, you know."

Mrs Abbot looked over at Simon with the chocolate now dripping down his chin. "Simon, I am so pleased to see that you are thinking about the importance of freedom.

Actually, I haven't thought about it for a long time but that is initially what drove me to want to become a lawyer. It may not seem like it now, as I don't have much freedom with my own work but freedom is exactly what being a lawyer is all about, protecting the rights and freedom of all people," she said and then she picked up a pen and signed the note.

*

For Emma it was easy. She had come home by bus and was feeling rather tired. Before settling on the couch to watch television, she put the permission form on the kitchen table and called out to her mum, "Need you to sign a permission form. Also might need some new party clothes!" Her mother read the notice with interest and looked over with pride at Emma, who was now sprawled out on the couch, eating her sandwich with Cooper, her dog, snuggled up next to her, already engrossed in her television program. Mrs Beaumont signed the notice and placed it in Emma's school bag.

Tuesday Morning: 12 April 2011

The day of the demonstration Seder arrived. Ms Nixon had reluctantly allowed the students to miss netball practice that afternoon after they had promised to practise during lunchtime. Mrs Leveson was waiting for them in her car when they walked out the gates. They were beside themselves with excitement. They had already changed into their party clothes. Simon was wearing a new T-shirt with 'Abercrombie' emblazoned on the front which his father had sent from Los Angeles. Emma's mum had taken her shopping to Surf Dive 'n' Ski and she was twirling around in a flared pink mini-skirt with a matching tank top. Talia had chosen a brightly coloured yellow floral dress from her wardrobe and tied up her hair with a matching ribbon. Maha stood self-consciously among them in her Vinnies clothes wearing the sports shoes that Talia had given her as her feet could no longer be squeezed into any of her other shoes. They all climbed into the car and chatted away happily as they were driven to Talia's house.

The tall figure of Mr Zulman stood waiting outside the gate and they were all ushered into the dining room by Mrs Leveson. They stood in the doorway for a moment stunned by the beautiful table setting. The bright red serviettes and purple and yellow roses contrasted with the starched white tablecloth. At the centre of the table stood the shining, silver Seder plate which looked far grander than when Mr Zulman had described it to them. The children settled themselves at the table and Mr Zulman began to speak, just a little self-consciously as Mrs Leveson hovered in the background.

"Today we come to celebrate the festival of Passover. We remember not only the suffering of the Israelite slaves in Egypt but of all people who have been oppressed and all those who continue to suffer. Passover is also a festival of freedom. We celebrate the release from slavery and the attainment of freedom of every person and nation and pray for the release of those who are still struggling to gain their liberty. We always start the Seder by inviting all those who are hungry and alone to join us. Let us drink four glasses of wine, or in your case grape juice, to show that we are free people and can sit and enjoy ourselves. The four glasses represent God's promise in the Bible to 'bring out, to deliver, to redeem and take out,' and we pray that this promise will also become true for those that are still suffering."

The children began to thirstily drink the red grape juice. Mr Zulman laughed, "You don't have to drink the four glasses in one go! It is also important to consider that our freedom often comes at the cost to others, so we are going to take out some of our wine to remember those that suffered as the result of the plagues. So each time that I call out a plague, you will dip your finger in the grape juice and remove some of the wine that symbolises our happiness."

The children were thrilled that they could dip their finger in the sticky grape juice and when Mr Zulman had finished calling out each plague, they licked their fingers with delight since surely no one could accuse them of having bad manners.

"Let us eat the matzah, the unleavened bread. As you might remember, the Israelites had to flee and did not have time to wait for the bread to rise. We also think of all those who have to hurriedly flee their countries in the search of freedom."

Mr Zulman noticed a shadow of sadness cross Maha's face but she was soon smiling again as they munched the crunchy matzo, the crumbs settling on their chins.

"Now we are going to place the charoset, the mixture of apples, nuts, cinnamon and wine, which represents the bricks that the slaves had to make, on top of the flat bread. As we eat, we think of all those who are still subject to enforced labour."

The children broke off pieces of matzo and spooned the apple mixture onto it and took bites, while still trying to talk to each other.

"Now dip the parsley into the salt water to recall the bitter tears of the slaves and the tears of people who still cry out in despair."

The children carefully dipped the parsley in the salt water and nibbled on the leaves, which was not quite to their taste.

"Prepare yourselves to eat the raw horseradish on the flat bread, the matzah, to remember the bitter suffering of the slaves and all those who have and still experience hardship."

The children gingerly took a bite of the horseradish and laughed at each other as they spluttered when the bitterness hit and tears came to their eyes. Mrs Leveson looked at Talia's smiling face and realised that she had never seen her child this happy. She was just about to get up to go and get the eggs in saltwater from the kitchen when the front doorbell rang. She went to open the door and they heard her saying, "Come in."

Maha froze as she heard the familiar rattle of bucket and mop.

"Carry on, just the cleaner," remarked Mrs Leveson as she turned to go to the kitchen.

As Maha's father passed the doorway, he stopped in his

tracks and their eyes locked. Embarrassment welling up in her, she lowered her eyes and she heard his retreating heavy footsteps as he made his way up the stairs. Mrs Leveson served the boiled eggs and salt water. Maha sat wracked with guilt. The sound of the vacuum cleaner upstairs hummed in her head and she caught only fragments of what Mr Zulman was saying.

Salt water for the tears... boiled egg...

The others looked at her curiously but did not say anything. The egg felt as if it was lodged in her throat. Suddenly she pushed back her chair and ran from the table. She made her way upstairs, silently took her father's hand and led him downstairs and into the dining room. All eyes turned to her. Mrs Leveson was astonished at the sight of Maha and her cleaner.

"This is my father," she announced quietly and turned to Mr Zulman.

"You know how you said at the beginning, all welcome..." Mr Zulman nodded wordlessly. "Can we invite Father to join us?"

Mrs Leveson, who by now had regained her composure, intervened, "Of course, everyone is welcome at our Seder. Please join us Ibrahim."

Her father looked at Maha with pride and turned to Mrs Leveson, "Thank you my daughter and you, Mrs Leveson, for the invitation but today I have work to finish."

He turned to Maha, "I too have been to a Seder many years ago when visiting a Jewish doctor friend in London. So Maha, no need for you to keep a secret when celebrating the holiday of freedom."

Maha coloured slightly and took her seat at the table.

Mr Zulman lifted his glass, "Mr Hassan, would you join us for a glass of wine, actually grape juice, to celebrate the freedom of all people?"

"That I will do with pleasure," he replied and lifted the newly filled glass. "To freedom of all people!"

And all the children lifted their glasses and shouted in unison, "Freedom!"

Friday Afternoon: 15 April 2011

The day of the netball finals had, at long last, arrived. When Ms Nixon had announced at the school assembly that the netball team was in the finals, there were yells of delight.

They were playing their archrivals Lindfield Park again. Unfortunately for the team, flu had gone around the school in the past week; they had enough players to fill the team but they had no reserves. As the team warmed up, parents and supporters began to gather around the court. Emma's mum and dad sat on the ground chatting to Mrs Leveson, who sat on her fold-up chair, immaculately dressed in her white linen shorts, pale blue silk shirt and a large straw sun hat that she always wore outdoors. Simon noticed with relief that his mother, although still in her black business suit, had managed to come. Mrs Abbot was busily checking her Blackberry. She looked up momentarily to give him the thumbs up. Simon hoped that she would stop working when the game began and watch the match. Only Maha's parents stood apart from the other spectators. Her mother was distinguishable from the others by the bright red scarf that covered her hair. Maha was concerned that her parents looked a little downcast but she was too excited to think about it and with the imminent start of the match, she went to take up her position.

Emma stood in the centre, holding the ball. As soon as the umpire blew the whistle, Emma threw the ball straight and hard to the wing attack and within seconds, the ball was in the hands of Maha, who aimed and scored the first goal of the match. Everyone cheered loudly and Maha smiled broadly, feeling excessively proud in front of her parents. The Lindfield Park centre took up the ball and they too swiftly scored their first goal. Everyone knew that this would be a hard-fought match. Each goal that Darlinghurst East scored was equalled by one from Lindfield Park. Simon defended as if his life depended on it but again the Lindfield Park defence was equally as good. By halftime the score was fifteen each and the team gathered around Ms Nixon to strategise, while Talia handed out the oranges.

The second half followed the same pattern as the first. Neither side could get ahead. Talia's voice was hoarse from screaming. The match was drawing to a close and it looked like a draw was inevitable. Emma jumped up to intercept a ball and as she caught it mid-air, her opponent collided

GS
GD

with her, knocking her off balance and she fell to the ground with her foot twisted underneath her. She groaned in agony, as she tried to stand up and her foot buckled. Talia ran to get the ice pack and Emma's parents came quickly onto the court and lifted her up. The spectators groaned as their best player was carried off the court.

Talia heard Ms Nixon's concerned voice saying, "No reserves, what are we going to do?" And then, "Talia, on the court!"

She felt a cold shiver run down her spine. She turned with fear to Ms Nixon. "You know that I can't catch a ball," she pleaded.

"We need you, there's nobody else!" responded Ms Nixon without much conviction and Talia saw the same doubt reflected on the faces of her friends. Talia was still in her school uniform and she looked down miserably at her school shoes. *I don't even have sports shoes,* she thought to herself.

She felt the strong hand of her mother on her shoulder, "Talia, you can do it!" She looked up into her mother's eyes and saw a look of complete and unwavering confidence. Talia walked hesitantly onto the court with the words of her mother ringing in her ears. She heard someone say, "Give her the ball. Maybe she can throw. She can't catch!" She felt the now-almost-forgotten yet familiar pain at the pit of her stomach. Ms Nixon handed her the ball at the spot where Emma had fallen. As if from a distance, she heard the sound of the whistle. She had watched the team practising the netball throw from the shoulder many times.

She heard her mother scream, "You can do it!" and thought to herself that she had never heard her mother shout. She lifted the ball to her shoulder and within the haze of darting players, she saw the face of Maha, hands outstretched and she threw the ball to her with all her might. And as if in slow motion, her feet rooted to the ground, she saw Maha catch the ball, aim and shoot. Everyone held their breath as the ball teetered on the edge of the ring for a second and then dropped in. Talia stood motionless with her heart beating rapidly as the final whistle sounded. She heard the shouts of joy from her teammates and their supporters as they surrounded her and hugged each other. She looked around for her mother who stood, arms folded, with a look of pure satisfaction on her face.

The teams began to line up for the presentation ceremony. Emma hobbled up, leaning heavily on her parents as her ankle had swelled up like a balloon. Talia was about to make her way to her usual place on the sideline when the team all called out for her to join them.

"You won the match for us!" shouted Simon.

Talia shook her head and said, "No, Emma won the season

for us," and the team cheered while Emma smiled weakly through her excruciating pain. The official congratulated both teams on their sportsmanship and excellent play and presented the cup to Emma. She lifted the shiny, silver cup in the air and everybody clapped loudly.

As soon as the ceremony was over, Simon, overjoyed that his mother had witnessed their victory and was still there, ran up to her and said, "Can we take the team out for a pizza to celebrate?"

She checked her Blackberry, hesitated, looked up to see his excited face and put the Blackberry back in her bag.

"Let's do it, parents included!" she said emphatically and Simon ran off to invite the team, who happily agreed.

He ran up to invite Maha, who was standing with her parents, "We are having a pizza celebration, are you coming?"

But before she could respond, her father intervened, "Sorry, we have an important family matter to discuss."

Maha was about to protest but saw her father's serious face. She masked her bitter disappointment and remained silent. Simon felt his elation evaporating and walked slowly away, knowing that the celebration would not be the same without Maha.

Tuesday Morning: 3 May 2011

Mr Zulman entered the room and immediately realised that something was amiss. The students were gathered around Maha, who was sobbing.

"What is the matter, Maha?" he asked, filled with concern.

Maha just continued to sob, unable to utter a word.

Emma answered for her. "The government says that Maha and her family have to go back to Iraq. Her father does not want to spend any more time fighting to stay in Sydney."

"And it's still very dangerous, bombs go off there every day!" added Talia.

Mr Zulman looked at them in stunned silence. He thought to himself, *their protection visas were obviously not granted.* He was filled with pity as he looked at Maha's bowed head as she gulped, trying to stifle her sobs.

"Mr Zulman," began Emma, "you know how we have been talking about slavery and oppression?" Mr Zulman nodded and Emma continued, "Well, wouldn't it be like sending Maha back into a kind of slavery? Don't we have to do something to stop it happening?"

He felt the children looking at him expectantly and Maha turned her tear-stained face towards him anxiously.

Mr Zulman was at a loss. "I'm not sure what we can do," he began slowly and, at that moment, felt that all his story telling of the past weeks was meaningless and that he had let his students down when they had placed their trust in him.

Suddenly Simon interrupted, "I know what we can do. I can phone my mum. She's a lawyer. She will know how to save Maha and her family. She will be our Moses," he finished with a flourish.

"When she gets home tonight I will tell her about it. I know that she will help you."

Maha dried her tears. The others began to relax and started telling Mr Zulman about their netball victory the previous week. Mr Zulman did not even attempt to teach them and sat, listening, since he was still very concerned about the welfare of Maha and her family. Despite Simon's certainty that his mother would help, he knew how difficult it would be to keep them in Australia.

Tuesday Afternoon

Simon went home directly after school and sat, waiting hour after hour for his mother. It was already dark when she finally returned home to find him asleep on the couch. He woke up with a start and was immediately wide awake.

"Mum," he began, "I have a very important problem to discuss with you."

Although his mother was exhausted, she sat down and looked at him concernedly.

"Maha and her family are being sent back to Iraq. She says that it is very dangerous for her and her family. But I told her not to worry because you are a lawyer and that you will fix it!"

She looked at him for a moment and said, "Simon, it is very late now. Perhaps we should discuss this in the morning."

"No, now!" said Simon with determination.

"Look, Simon, I am deeply sorry for Maha and her family but I am a corporate lawyer. My clients are companies, not refugees. I don't know anything about immigration law. So I really don't think I can help them."

Simon's face turned white with rage, which highlighted his freckles and he screamed at her, "I never ask you for anything! I sit in this empty apartment day after day, all alone and never complain. I ask you one time only for your help and you straight out refuse. I hate you! I'm going to live with Dad!" and he stormed off to his room, slamming the door behind him.

Tuesday Morning: 10 May 2011

Mr Zulman walked slowly into the classroom, his forehead creased in a concerned frown. Talia and Emma were in deep conversation with Simon and Mr Zulman noticed that Emma handed Simon a bag. Maha was absent. As soon as they realised that he had arrived, they quickly took their seats, being careful to avoid eye contact with him.

"I take it that you know that Maha has disappeared."

He paused and no one looked at him.

"Her parents are beside themselves with worry."

Still they did not look at him.

"If you have any idea where she may be, you need to let her family know."

He knew that no teaching would be possible.

"Perhaps you would like to take the rest of this class to consider your options." No one moved, not even Talia. They sat in an uneasy silence for the remainder of the class. As soon as the bell rang, they all jumped up and ran out without a backward glance. He heard Simon say, "To the rooftop!" and they disappeared out of sight.

Tuesday Afternoon

Simon walked quickly towards home. He stopped at Mr Naidoo's shop and walked straight in.

"Smells like fresh samousas," he said to Mrs Naidoo and smiled.

"Would you like one, Simon?" she asked.

"Actually, I'm really hungry today. Would it be OK if I took two?"

"Certainly," replied Mr Naidoo. "For a growing boy, take more," which Simon did as his face turned bright red.

"Sit down and relax," said Mr Naidoo.

"Unfortunately, I am in a bit of a hurry, so I will just take them with me. Thank you," said Simon and he hurried out of the shop. Simon struggled to open the front door to his apartment while trying to balance the samousas and the key.

"Maha!" he shouted. "It's only me. I've got food and clothing for…" and stopped mid-sentence.

Sitting in his lounge looking very solemn were his mother, Mr Zulman, Maha's parents and Maha with a tear-stained face.

"You betrayed us!" he shouted heatedly at Mr Zulman. "So much for teaching us about freedom and helping what you always call 'the oppressed'."

"That's enough!" interceded his mother. "We understand what you and your friends were trying to do but how do you think Maha's parents have been feeling these last few days?"

"It's easy to hide someone in a big, *empty* apartment," he retorted bitterly.

His mum was silent for a moment. "Actually, Simon, I have been working around the clock to aid Maha and her parents to stay in Australia."

Simon's face lit up. "I knew that you would come good," he said with an embarrassed smile.

"Simon, I said that I am trying, no promises. Let's all calm down and have a cup of tea."

While the adults sat around drinking tea and examining documents, Simon and Maha ate the samousas and waited.

Tuesday Morning: 15 May 2011

As Mr Zulman entered the classroom, his heart sank. Maha was not present and the three others sat in dismal silence. Mr Zulman knew without a word being said that Simon's mother had been unsuccessful. He sat down heavily in his chair. For the first time in his life, he had no story to tell. Emma and Talia looked at him with tears in their eyes while Simon tried to choke back his. All Mr Zulman could do was to try and comfort his distraught students.

"Let us not forget that the Israelites had given up hope when Moses came to save them," he said.

His words sounded hollow even to himself.

Suddenly the door swung open. Mrs Abbot rushed in, saying, "I have permission from the Minister for them to stay in Australia! Where are they?"

"At the airport," the children shouted in unison, jumping out of their seats.

"Quick. No time to spare. My car is outside."

Ignoring school rules they all left the classroom and headed immediately to the school car park. Mrs Abbot's high heels and tight skirt did not hinder her as she started running towards the car, followed closely by Mr Zulman, Talia, Simon and Emma, who still limped slightly, moving as fast as she could so as not to be left behind. They all climbed into the car, which lunged forward as they sped off towards the airport.

Mrs Abbot weaved between lanes, disregarding the speed limits and swearing under her breath at the state of Sydney traffic. Simon had never seen his mother drive like that and would have enjoyed the ride if he was not so concerned for his friend. They pulled up at the entrance to the airport with a screech, discarding the car in the 'no stopping' zone and ran inside. He had never seen his mother disobey so many laws.

"Which airline? Which airline?" she muttered under her breath as she desperately scanned the departure board. "Must be Arab Emirates. It's about to depart. Run, run!" she urged them.

They weaved their way through the crowds following Mrs Abbot, fear gripping their hearts. She ran up to the Arab Emirates desk that was now empty except for an attendant tidying some papers.

The children and Mr Zulman ran to the window,

squinting against the midday sun at the white aeroplane on the tarmac and the word 'Emirates' in large black letters confirming that this was the plane that held captive their friend and her family. They saw the stairs being pulled up and Simon groaned as the heavy doors were slammed shut. They heard in the background the voice of Mrs Abbot getting louder and louder with desperation, "I demand that you stop the flight, immediately!" The plane began to move slowly forward towards the runway. Talia wept softly. They did not turn when Mrs Abbot joined them at the window and they watched as the plane slowly lifted upwards.

They stood motionless, eyes transfixed until the red, green and black tail of the plane was just a fading speck in the cloudless Sydney sky.

The End